PETER KELLY

ONLY A FOOL SLEEPS IN THE SHADOW OF A CAMEL'S BACK

First edition

This book was professionally typeset on Reedsy.
Find out more at reedsy.com

For the broad-shouldered giants that came before.

If a man knows not to which port he sails, no wind is favourable. It is not because things are difficult that we do not dare; it is because we do not dare that things are difficult. Find a path or make one.

It's all in your head; you have the power to make things seem hard or easy or even amusing. If we let things terrify us, life will not be worth living. Laugh at your problems; everybody else does. You are your choices, and the choice is yours.

Seneca the Younger

Contents

Acknowledgement

Much love to everyone who's helped me on this journey so far. In the words of John Squire and Liam Gallagher, I know you know who you are.

And here's to those who bore us. And made us what we are.

FENCING OFF FANNIES

Honest tae god, this is absolute pish. Pure Chernobyl-orange, rancid pish. It's bad enough ma maw made me stay oan at school. It's a kick in the staines she made me take this poncy fuckin joab as well.

'Happy birthday, son,' she telt me a month ago. 'Now away and see Davey Dunnit round the corner. He's gonny get ye a wee part-time job in his DIY shop.'

To be fair, she probably never called him Davey Dunnit. Because that's no his name. It's Davey Caldwell, but most folk call him Davey Dunnit as no matter wit you've done, he's done it anaw. Only better. You've been tae Tenerife? He's been tae Elevenerife.

And it's no his DIY shop either. It's no even a shop. It's fuckin Homebase. Forty-odd year-old n he's mixin paint for snobby pricks, n cuttin timber for cunts too tight tae hire a joiner. Ah'd wager the only reason he got me this joab is cause he's gaggin for a ride at ma maw. Guaranteed if ma da done a bunk, he'd be straight at the door dressed in his best jeans n suit-jacket combo, reekin ay Old Spice, hair strategically placed n drenched in Just For Men, and carrying a bunch ay flowers lookin like they've spent the last two weeks tied tae a lampost.

So ah telt ma maw, 'Ah'm no wantin a joab.'

She came back wae some pishy parent-patter like, 'Wit you want and wit you get are two completely different things, Charles.'

Ah would've likely hit her wae some witty comeback like, 'Good wan,

1

maw.'

Then she played her ace in the hole.

'Well, ma boy,' she said, crossin her arms wae a smug look oan her face. 'You'd better make that birthday money last, because now yer a man, the pocket money stops.'

Ah telt her that sixteen isnae a man.

She came back wae some good-auld-days shite aboot how she wis up the chimneys when she wis twelve.

This led us intae a debate aboot exactly when adulthood begins. Normally, I'd argue it's the moment ye sprout yer first curly hair, but for financial reasons, ah wis trying tae downplay ma manhood.

She then hit us wae the auld enough tae leave school, get yer ain hoose, marry, have sex, vote, n join the army pish.

Even though leavin school n having sex is actually quite appealin, ah fired straight back wae, 'Ah'm only allowed tae get married or join the army wae *your* consent, and if ah'm noo considered an adult, how come ah cannae drink?'

Big mistake arguing the drinkin age as she then pointed oot that ah'd been drinkin for the last year.

Took aw ma willpower tae keep fae tellin her how wrang she wis – it's actually closer tae two years.

In a last ditch attempt, ah pleaded tae the rational half ay ma parents. That pussy-whipped bitch just goes, 'No point in arguing, son. Yer mum knows best.'

So here ah am. Every single fuckin school night. Fae dinner time tae kick-off in the Europa League matches. Stackin shelves n helpin dittery auld bastards choose wit kinda screws wid be best for hangin pictures of their mutant grandweans. Meanwhile, aw ma mates are playing FIFA or havin a toke doon the park.

Wit's the point in workin aw the hours under the sun if ye don't get the time tae enjoy the fruits ay yer labour? Ah hope whoever invented this workin for a livin pish is gettin a rid-hot poker rammed up his shitter fae a rid-skinned, pointy-bearded guy wae horns n hooves as we speak.

'*Customer assistance required at the paint mixer. Customer Assistance at the paint mixer,*' Davey Dunnit announces in his talking-to-the-traffic-cops-while-under-the-influence voice.

They must be busy wae Christmas shoppers at the front if that trouser stain's oan the tills. No that I'd know as ah spend most ay ma time here hiding like a drug baron in Spain. Ye see, if ye hang aboot the builders section, ye generally get left alone. The customers that buy fae these aisles usually know exactly wit they're after, and don't need tae ask a wee dick wae a name badge for advice.

Plus, this bit is right next tae the garden centre, which means there's a good chance ay gettin a wee gander at Natalie if she's oan. She usually works the weekend, but on the odd occasion when ma luck's in, she'll take an evenin shift. Ah clocked her as soon as ah came in the night – waterin the indoor plants like a goddess.

What an absolute wee pump she is. She wis the year above me at school, and ah think ah've had a wee thing for her from the moment ah set eyes oan her. There's somethin aboot aulder women that's so alluring. Although, doubt ah'll still think that when ah'm in ma thirties. She reminds me ay that Khaleesi bird fae *Game ay Thrones*. Golden blonde hair. Pale skin ye just know is softer than marshmallows sprinkled wae baby powder. Light-blue eyes that turn yer legs tae jelly. A cute wee smile tinged wae naughtiness that makes yer heart beat like an old-skool, happy-harcdore dance tune, n ah'm no even gonny *begin* describing her tits n arse for fear ay gettin a stawner. Gettin a wee keek at her now n again almost makes aw this pish worthwhile.

So here ah am – trying tae look busy by facing up the shelves, while sneakin peeks at ma socials tae see wit the troops are uptae, n wishin ah wis any fuckin where but here.

'*Customer Assistance at the paint mixer. Customer assistance at the paint mixer.*'

Davey Dunnit's voice carries a wee hint ay annoyance this time. I'm guessing no cunt's answered his first call, n the customer's giving him pelters. Good enough for him, the prick, and they can go fuck a duck if they think ah'm gonny help a punter that's awready pissed aff.

Ah glance up as the automatic doors tae the garden centre open – quickly divertin ma gaze when Natalie steps inside. From the corner ay ma eye, she stops, glances around, before headin towards me wae a customer in tow.

She's saying, 'Not too sure, but my colleague should be able tae help.'

Fuck! Unless that customer wants tae know how tae open a bottle ay beer withoot a bottle opener, or who the premiership's top scorer wis last season, she's onto plums.

They reach me n ah turn as if ah've just noticed them – casual as fuck, like.

'Hi Charles,' she says wae a wee smile that instantly dries ma mooth.

Ah moisten ma lips. 'H-how dae you know ma name?'

Her eyes are like a punch in the belly when they drap tae ma name badge for a split second.

What a *dick*.

The customer beside her starts laughin hard. 'Fuck me,' he says, 'who ordered the extra large portion ay cringe wae red-face sauce?' The prick looks me up n doon wae a wee sneer oan his face before cuppin his hawns over his mooth. 'Clean up in aisle ten. Bring a big mop – there's dignity been spilt everywhere.'

Natalie has an awkward look oan her face as her eyes dart between me n this tadger beside her, laughin in ma face. He looks at least early twenties, n is decked oot in a black n white Moschino tracky, topped off wae a Gucci hat.

'Aw, no way hosay!' this walkin advert for abortions says as he rubs

4

his hawns in front ay ma face. 'Who turnt the heatin up?' His fake Rolex jingles n jangles before ma eyes. 'Taxi for a wee guy wae a beamer!'

The heatwave ay embarrassment gets overtaken by the inferno ay rage. Ah open ma mouth, but Natalie beats me tae the punch.

'Charles,' she says, 'I was just saying to John—'

'Call me Jokey, darlin,' cunt-face says. 'Aw ma pals do. Jokeyboy69, that's ma handle on aw ma socials.'

Natalie stares at him wae a look on her face as cold as a Greggs sausage roll before turning back tae me. 'Can you help John with…' she turns back tae Joke the Coke and raises her brow.

'Cement, darlin,' wank-breath says, flashing her a wink. He looks at me. 'Ye see, *wee* man, I'm wantin a jacuzzi tae put oan the deckin ah'm getting oot ma back, but ah'm no wantin aw ma nosey bastardin neighbours seeing wit ah get uptae in there, know wit ah mean?' He steals a glance at Natalie who's staring at him as if he's a kettle boilin. 'Ah thought aboot stickin it in ma summer hoose when it gets here, but ah'm wantin tae turn that intae a bar n stick a pool table in it, know wit ah'm gettin at?'

Oh, ah know *exactly* wit you're gettin at, Joke, the dry boak. 'So…wit ye after then?'

'Cement for the fence posts ah'm gonny put up aroon ma jacuzzi.'

'Who's doin yer deckin?'

'Just a couple ay boys that owe us a couple ay favours, know wit ah mean?'

I know that Joke the Clown's words spewing fae his lips live uptae his name. 'Why don't ye get they boys tae do it while they're doin yer deckin? If they're able tae lay deckin, a fence should be nae bother.'

Big Joke's punchable face draps as his eyes dart tae Natalie. She's starin at him wae her eyes narrowed n head tilted. It looks like she's tryin tae keep fae smilin.

'Eh…' he says, '…ah would do, but ah like doin as much DIY as possible.

5

Pretty hands-on guy, me.'

'Cool,' ah say, noddin n strokin ma chin. 'Well, wit kinda grun have ye got?'

'Eh?'

'The ground ye'll be puttin the fence posts in. Wit kind is it?'

He snorts. 'It's grass.'

'Aye, but wit's underneath it?'

The butt-plug enthusiast glances at Natalie wae a bewildered look on his glaikit face before back at me. 'Dirt, ya maddy.'

'Aye, but wit *kind* ay dirt?'

'Wit dae ye mean?'

'Is it dark brown or light brown? Is it clay or sand? Is it waterlogged or drier than an Arab's sandal? Is it full ay stones or finer than Peruvian flake? Is it aw the same or is it differing layers? Is it full ay worms and insects, or is it the type more suited tae moles?'

'Eh, to be honest'—there's a first time for everythin—'ah'm no too sure, pal.'

So we're pals now?

Ah give him that look tradesmen give right before answerin the question – how much is this gonny cost? 'If ye don't even know wit kinda soil the posts'll be goin intae, maybe ye should leave the men's work tae the professionals.'

His face twists intae a blend ay anger n offence. 'Wit you tryin tae say?'

'Ah'm no "*tryin*" tae say anythin.'

Jokeyboy69's eyes narrow as he glares at me. Ah keep ma expression as casual as a Millwall supporter while holdin his gaze.

Natalie jumps in and says, 'I think Charles is just trying to make sure ye get the right stuff ye need, Jokey.'

'*Charles Mcleod to the paint mixer immediately. Charles Mcleod to the paint mixer.*'

6

Natalie breathes a sigh of relief. 'Charles, you'd better answer that call. I'll see to—'

'Ohhh, no, no, no,' ah say tae Natalie while keepin ma eyes locked on the tool in front ay me. 'Not at all. I'm no leavin here until this cuntstomer's a happy one.'

'Did you just call me a cun—'

'Well...' says Natalie, '...is there anything that works on *all* types of soil?'

'Of course there is,' ah say.

'Well, what is it then?'

'Postcrete. It's right there,' ah say, pointing tae the pallet.

'Brilliant,' Natalie says wae a wee hint ay relief in her voice. 'Jokey, me and Charles will go get a trolley for you.'

Jokeyboy69 turns to Natalie. 'Actually, darlin, ah'll no be taking any the day. Ah'm here in the BM an ah'm no wantin tae get it boggin. Plus, as it's the sports model, ah'm no even sure there's enough room in the boot. Ah'll be back wae wan ay ma pals vans. Cheers for yer help, doll.'

Jokeyboy69 has one last growl at me before shoulder bargin me as he swaggers past.

That inferno ay rage returns, n ah spin aroon.

Just as ah'm about tae give Jokeyboy69 an earful, Natalie puts a hand on ma shoulder, instantly dousin the flames. Ah turn n look intae her mesmerising eyes.

'I know how ye feel,' she whispers, 'but he's no worth it. When he said about no having enough room in his motor, I had tae stop myself saying – why don't ye put them between yer ears? There's plenty of room there.'

I laugh.

'I take it all that stuff about the soil was to show him up for the prick he is?'

I nod, tryin tae suppress a smirk. 'A wee bit.'

She smiles n it feels like ma birthday, Christmas, and that time Stacey Barr flashed her tits tae aw the boys at the smokin corner for a fag oafy each ay us, all rolled intae one.

'Tell me,' ah say, 'does aw that flash-git pish appeal tae lassies?'

She shrugs. 'It does to some, I guess.'

'That's a relief cause wae the pay in here, it'll take me years tae afford wan ay that clown's trainers.'

Natalie smiles. 'Is that three weeks ye've been workin here now? How are ye liking it?'

'As much as double history wae Mr Slater.'

'God, that brings back memories. I'm *so* glad I got outta there as soon as I could. College is *so* much better. You were the year below me, right?'

It's like a fountain ay joy eruptin inside at the revelation she does know me. 'Eh, aye, ah thinkso. You were in Hendo and Tonto's year, no?'

She nods. 'Are you still there?'

'Unfortunately. Ma maw said if ah didnae have a job or college place ah wis stayin on tae do fifth year. Fuckin nazi.'

'She just wants what's best for her wee boy, Charles.'

'It's Chaz,' ah blurt oot afore realisin how much ah sound like Jokeyboy69.

She smiles n hawds oot her hand.

Ah discreetly dry ma palms oan ma trousers before takin it. It's like stickin yer finger intae a socket the moment we connect.

'Nice to meet you, Chaz. I'm Natalie, but all ma pals call me...Natalie!'

We both laugh, still holdin hands. Jesus, please make this las—

'There ye are!'

I drop Natalie's hand n we both spin in the direction ay the voice. Davey Dunnit looking like he's got a bee in his bunnet marches along the aisle towards us.

8

'Here comes the fuhrer,' ah whisper.

'Don't...' Natalie says wae a wee laugh.

Davey Dunnit's glarin right at me. 'Did ye not hear the call to the paint mixer? Or were ye too busy chatting up your co-workers?' He reaches us, stops, n puts his hawns on his hips. 'Twenty minutes those customers waited for their paint to be mixed. Let me tell you, they were *not* happy campers.'

'Charles was busy helping me with another customer, Davey.'

'Oh aye,' Davey Dunnit says, theatrically glancin around. 'Was it the invisible man?'

'Don't be daft,' Natalie says. 'He's literally just left.'

'Convenient. Look, ah was the same as yous once. Just outta school with no idea how to get on in this world. Ah fannied about like yerselves, before realising the only way to make something of yerself is to stick in, work hard, and do a good job. Look at me now – assistant manager with a nice wee hoose and a decent motor.'

'Thanks for the advice, Davey,' Natalie says. 'We're really sorry and promise it won't happen again.'

Davey seems pleased his wisdom has been emparted, but even an inexperienced wee guy like myself can tell Natalie's words were barely even lip service.

'So,' Davey Dunnit says, 'what were yous gossiping about? Better no have been me.'

'Nah,' I say, 'this joab's borin enough.'

Natalie chortles a wee laugh before cuppin her mouth n pretend coughing.

Davey Dunnit scowls. 'I wonder what yer mum would think of that after me gettin you this job.'

'Ah'm only joking, Davey, I absolutely love it here. It's an absolute barrel ay laughs. Excitement galore. In fact, ah wis just tellin Natalie aboot a shoplifter ah saw earlier.'

Natalie looks at me, confused.

Ah give her a look saying play along. 'Remember?'

'Oh, aye,' she says, shakin her head. 'Terrible, just terrible.'

'Why, what happened?' Davey Dunnit says.

One annoying manager hooked. Time tae reel him in. 'Ah saw a guy in the garden centre stealin a gate.'

'Really? What did ye do?'

'Nothin.'

'Nothing! Why not?'

'Because ah didnae want him takin a fence.'

Natalie bursts oot laughin – it takes Davey Dunnit a moment before the penny drops.

'Aye, good one,' he says as his face turns red. 'Back to work before I take offence at your lack of commitment to this job and tell your mum.'

Davey Dunnit skulks away. Natalie smiles at me before turnin n headin back towards the garden centre. After only a few steps, she stops n turns. Ah quickly avert ma gaze from her arse.

'You'll know James McClure and Alan Young and that, won't ye?'

'Aye, ah'm quite pally wae they boys – they're sound as fuck. Why?'

'Tam Muir said James is having a gaff this Saturday. He invited me along.'

Tam Muir? There's another flash prick 'Wit, as in like a date?'

She smiles. 'No, I'll be going with ma pals. Will you be there?'

Ah fuckin will be now! 'Ehm...aye, ah might do. Ah've no made ma mind up yet. *Sooo* many options on the table.'

She smirks. 'Is that right?'

Ah nod, trying tae look as casual as can be.

'Well, I'll maybe see ye there, then.' She turns n walks away. 'If you grace us with yer presence, that is.'

The rest ay ma shift flies in, so much so, ah don't even check ma mobile buzzin away in ma pocket. Ma minds elsewhere. It's oan Natalie, n Jamsie's gaff. It's oan Natalie, n wit ah'll wear tae Jamsie's gaff. It's oan Natalie, n wit carry-oot ah'll get for Saturday – somethin sophisticated like Grey Goose or Cîroc. It's oan Natalie, n how it'll play out oan Saturday – aw the witty one liners ah'll say that'll have her drippin like a knackered fridge. Did ah mention ma mind's oan Natalie?

As ah'm walking home, ah finally pull ma phone oot tae see wit the troops are uptae. Ah can not *wait* tae tell them aboot work the night.

Ah unlock ma phone. Right there, stickin oot like a sore thumb at the top ay the notification bar, is a text fae ma gran. Ma world collapses when ah open it and read the message.

> *Hiya son it's your gran here.*
> *Your favourite one!*
> *Just checking we are still on*
> *for our wee xmas day out on*
> *Saturday. I'm helping at the fete*
> *at the community centre in the*
> *morning and early afternoon but*
> *will be ready to go for the train*
> *about 3 oclock. I'm looking forward*
> *to it but don't tell your cousins!*
> *This is our wee special day.*
> *Love from gran xxx*

Ah fuckin *hate* ma life.

ANSWERS AT THE BOTTOM OF A GLASS

'Rough day?' I say to the man hunched over his drink on the opposite side of the bar.

He lifts his bloodhound eyes. 'Rough life,' he says, deadpan, before downing his amber potion.

Jeez, this guy's lower than a miner's lunchbox. 'Same again?'

He nods and slides his glass towards me.

Picking a second glass from below the bar, I scoop both into the ice bucket, turn, and fill them from the gantry – a measure of whisky and amaretto in each. As I stir his drink, I consider him through the mirror running the full length of the bar.

He looks to be in his forties with thinning, greying hair, and thick glasses. His round, unshaven face is mapped with broken veins, and his double chin prominent due to his slouched demeanour. His cheap charcoal-suit looks like it's trying to flee from him, and his tie hangs loose, five inches from where it should sit. Not the type who'd have the ladies beating a path to his door. Perhaps that's what's getting him down. Whatever the case, he seems like a man who's been kicked square in the balls by life. The kind of man who works a dead-end job he tells everyone he loves – because it pays well, with a decent pension – but inside, he's slowly suffocating. He's the type I'd so often come across in here. The type I'm on this earth to deal with.

I sit his glass next to him, keeping hold of it by the rim. He makes to take it and glances up when I don't release it. His face is stony but a fire burns in his dark eyes.

'On the house,' I say. '*If* I can join you.'

'Are you allowed to drink on the job?'

Ahh, a stickler for the rules. No wonder he looks so downtrodden. 'Well first of all, it's my place, so I can do what I want. Second, it's near closing time. Doubt I'll get any more business tonight.'

He nods.

I release my grip, pull my stool over, and sit. 'So—'

'Is this the bit where you ask me what's up, I rabbit on telling you about how depressing my life is, you periodically nod and say things like "ahh" and "I see" while trying to look interested until I'm unburdened and you feel like a good Samaritan for listening?'

Wow. That was intense. Wasn't expecting that from him. His eyes – still locked on mine – seem to bore right through me.

'Or,' I say, 'we can just sit in silence. Up to you, pal.'

I sip my drink and he lowers his gaze back to his own. We sit in silence for a couple of minutes before he relents. They always do.

'It's my job,' he says, shaking his head. 'It's suffocating the life from me.'

I *knew* it.

'*Hang-ing on in qui-et des-pe-ra-tion is the Eng-lish way,*' I sing.

His eyes meet mine and for the first time a flicker of emotion curls his lips. 'Pink Floyd?'

I nod. 'It's a common thing, pal, from my experience anyway. You'd be surprised at the amount of people trapped working jobs they hate... so they can buy things they don't need, with money they don't have, to impress people they don't like.'

'Now you're quoting *Fight Club*,' he says as his face breaks into a smile. Actually, it's more of a smirk. Like the delirious soldier who's seen too many things. 'A real fountain of pop-culture knowledge you are.'

13

I smile. 'Am I right, though?'

He sighs and nods in agreement as his shoulders slump. 'More than you know.'

I smile inside when he takes a large drink. That-a-boy, numb that pain.

'You see,' he continues, 'my job's a thankless one. One I never even wanted in the first place. But no one else was willing to do the dirty work, so I stepped up, as without me, the venture would fail quicker than a sand factory in the desert.'

'So, it's a start-up?'

He considers this for a moment. 'It was...a long, long time ago. Yet here I am, still in the role I was promised would only be temporary until someone more suitable came along.' He shakes his head. 'The boss sure pulled a fast one on me.'

'That's rough, man,' I say, as sympathetic as I can muster. 'What is it you do?'

'I'm the Devil.'

I near choke with laughter.

He doesn't find it so amusing. 'Have you any idea how soul-destroying it is every time someone laughs at your job?'

'I'd have thought soul-destroying would be right up your street,' I say between laughs.

His face remains expressionless.

'I've got to say, pal,' I say, drying my eyes. 'That's the first I've heard that one.'

'Just because I'm the Devil doesn't mean I'm lying.' There's a cold, matter-of-factness behind his words that would freeze...well, his home.

I think the professionals would class him as a grade A nutter. Better play along. 'Sorry pal, I see where you're coming from. You do get a bad rap.'

He seems to relax as he sips his drink. 'Yeah, that's the point.

Everyone thinks *I'm* the bad one, but if they could see what I've got Jimmy Saville doing right now, they'd think differently. But oh-no, the gaffer wants me to play the bogeyman role. In fact, he actively promotes it. Says it keeps the sheep in check. So, I'm forever cursed to be the proverbial wolf at the door...the serpent in the garden...the barbarian at the wall.'

Now, I'm no mind reader or expert on body language, but I'd say this guy truly believes he's the Devil. Not long now and I won't have to listen to his ramblings. Soon, he'll be face-planted on the bar.

'Anyway,' he says, before finishing his drink. 'You're a busy man. I don't want to waste any more of your time listening to my...*ramblings*. Besides, you and I will have plenty of time to chat. All eternity, to be precise.'

I snigger. This guy's cuckoo. I'll enjoy this one.

'I really appreciate you taking the time to listen to a cuckoo like me,' he says. 'I'll have a word with the big man, but I'm not sure it'll be enough to get you off the hook.'

Cuckoo? I force a smile. 'I'm going to hell, am I?'

His eyes narrow in on me. 'You really need to ask that, Eddie?'

How the *fuck* does he know my name?

'Because I'm the Devil. I know everything about you, Eddie. Your name, age, where you live.' A sleekit smile crosses his face. 'I even know all the seedy ways you get your kicks.'

His whole demeanour changes as a light-headedness sweeps over me. He seems taller, confident, and an overwhelming sense of power radiates from him. The room sways, causing me to feel unsteady. I open my mouth, but no words come out.

What in the actual fuck is happening?

'Oh, I think you know very well what's happening, Eddie. The same thing that's happened to many-a-man unfortunate enough to drown their sorrows in here. First, it's a friendly chat with a sympathetic

15

barman. Then it's a free drink. Followed by drowsiness. Before finally – black. Next thing they know, they've woken in a ditch with no recollection of getting there, and it's at least a week before they can sit down properly. But how long does it take for what you do to them when you've drugged them to sit okay in their minds?'

The room spins and sweat floods my brow. I close my eyes and rub them with trembling hands. When I open them, I'm alone with only a slight puff of smoke before me, and a whiff of sulphur in the air.

This is surreal.

I glance at the two glasses on the bar, trying to figure out what's happening, but my panicked mind won't string a rational thought together.

But I...but I...

'But I don't understand?' comes the echoing voice of the vanished man. I turn as my breathing becomes laboured but still can't see him. 'But I spiked *his* drink? Those are the wrong butts I'd be thinking about. If I were you, I'd be worrying about protecting my own. God knows who could walk through that door when you're passed out.'

The room spins faster as my heart beats quicker, all the while, his malicious taunts echo around the bar. Echo, around my head.

'*Tick, tock, the door needs locked. Tick, tock, or you'll take a fat cock...*'

Chest tight with fear, I scramble over the bar sending the glasses smashing to the ground. I land and my legs buckle at the knees. I manage to crawl halfway to the door before my arms collapse under my weight. With the last energy I can muster, I roll onto my back. I struggle to lift my head but it's like fighting against the centrifugal force of the waltzers fairground ride at full spin. I give up and let my head thump onto the floor as the door bangs open. Through narrowing vision, a group of hairy-arsed bikers tower over me. My eyelids become too heavy to keep open but my ears still work fine.

'Any of you boys order a passed-out barman?' one of them says.

The others laugh.

'Well, I guess it's true what they say,' he continues. 'The lord *does* work in mysterious ways.'

A sickening symphony of twisted laughter, high-fives, belts being undone, zips opening, and my own heart pounding against my eardrums, lulls me into darkness.

DIFFERENT BATTLEGROUND; SAME WAR

Ahhh, breakfast with the family. Pure bliss.

I peer over the top of my Sunday broadsheet. My wife, Sandra, holds a mug of tea close to her chest like a poker player with all the aces. She leans, wide-eyed and smirking, over her *Woman* magazine lying open on the table. Must be a funny story. Or a raunchy one.

Jack, my eldest, is busy defying gender stereotypes as he swipes through his phone with one hand, while the other shovels food into his mouth. He's wearing that sullen expression teenagers love so much.

Ellie, my youngest, ignores her bowl of soggy wheat-cereal in favour of her tablet. Her brown curly-locks bounce like Slinkies as she bobs her head to some awful tune on her Spotify playlist.

'Ellie,' I say, getting no response. I chap the table in front of her. She looks up, bug-eyed, and pulls one of her earbuds out. 'Eat up, darling.'

She smiles, picks up her spoon, and pretends to eat.

I lower my gaze toward my paper, doing a bit of pretending myself. It's not long before she sneakily sets her spoon down and starts bobbing her head as she taps and swipes at her tablet.

I smile and shake my head. How things have changed since I was a child at the breakfast table.

It used to be nine of us crammed together in a room half the size of this one. My dad hungover from the pub the night before. Mum giving him the silent treatment for the state he was in, and the rest of us bickering, bordering on full-blown fighting.

The first fight was over the good seats. Just like in the jungle, the biggest and strongest got first dibs. Even if you sat down first, they'd just pick you up and dump you on the floor. The rest of us had to share. One cheek each was the agreed territory. Any border incursions were met with jagged elbows or cries of, 'Mum! they're pushing me off the chair.' Mum usually ended up with one or two of us upon her lap.

The second fight was over the food. Not that we didn't have enough to go around, but it wasn't the gluttonous portions of today. Back then, nothing went in the bin. Turning your back on your plate was as unwise as letting your wife go for drinks with Bill Cosby. A keen eye and sharp wit were needed to keep wandering hands at bay. Ellie wouldn't have lasted a minute. The moment she glanced at her tablet her bowl would've been emptied faster than she could say, 'Alexa, which local cafes deliver?'

Our meal times were better than any soap or reality TV show aired today. There always seemed to be one drama or the other unfolding. Whether it was one of us who had gotten into trouble with the police, or the dreaded letter from school, the sound of the postman was met with guilty faces and bated breath.

'What's going on with you and that Spiersy?' Jack says, looking at his sister with a furrowed brow.

I lower my paper and Sandra sits her mug down. Her eyes narrow and dart between her two kids.

'Nothing,' Ellie says sheepishly. She picks up her spoon and fidgets with it.

'That's not what Aiden just told me,' Jack says. He pauses, waiting for a reply that doesn't come. 'He says that wee idiot's been noiseing you up on Facebook.'

Ellie stares into her bowl, stirring the mush. 'It's fine.'

It wasn't fine. A blindfolded bat could see that.

'Ellie,' I say, capturing her attention. 'If someone's bothering you, you can tell us. You won't be in any trouble.'

'It's cool, Dad,' Jack says. 'I'll sort him out.'

I glance at Sandra. She raises her eyebrows. I give her a reassuring nod.

I know I shouldn't condone any "sorting out", but I'd be lying if I said I wasn't proud of my son for sticking up for his sister. It is, after all, a big brother's duty to look out for his siblings. I snigger to myself as a similar situation from my childhood comes to mind.

I must've been around twelve at the time, kicking about the streets in trousers too short and full of holes, and shoes you could have used as a puppet. Not that anyone cared. None of us kicked about in designer trainers back then. Anyone who did, wouldn't have had them for very long.

Me and my pals were playing football on the road outside our tenement. Would have been commie or heady-two-touch, with jumpers used as goalposts. We'd play for hours without needing to step aside for a car, and when we did, the driver got growled at for interrupting our game. It's likely I was winning – running rings around everyone and scoring goals Archie Gemmill would've been proud of – when I heard my name being called in a way that meant one thing – trouble.

A wee boy in the year below me at school sprinted through the close of our tenement. I can't remember his name, but he palled about with my wee sister Angela. I'm pretty sure they were in the same class.

'Jimmy! Jimmy!' He shouted. 'You'd better come quick. A boy's hitting your Angela.'

Game abandoned. I sprinted to him. 'Where are they?'

He stood aside and pointed through the close. 'Out the back.'

I ran past him thinking who the fuck's ballsy enough to batter my Angela when I'm on the other side of the building? Shrill screams of 'No!' and 'Stop!' seeped into the close. The red mist descended. My legs wouldn't go fast enough and my fists clenched. He was getting it.

I barrelled out the back door, and if your life truly does flash before your eyes in your last moments, that scene will be presented in HD. It still buckles me to this day.

In the centre of a ring of baying weans was my eleven-year-old sister and her tormentor. She had the nameless bully in a headlock, raining punches on his head, ten to the dozen.

Someone in the crowd shouted, 'There's Jimmy, you're really in for it now.'

The boy begged me to make her stop. Angela looked up at me with a look that said, 'Come ahead.'

Now, I've been in enough scraps over the years to know when it's best to walk away. I laughed and headed back to resume my game of football. Cries of 'Jimmy! Help!' from my wee sister's punch bag followed me through the close.

Departing memory lane, I realise Jack hasn't moved a muscle since declaring his intent to defend his sister. He's still at the table, swiping away at his phone. When's he planning on doing this sorting out? I'd already be halfway round to this Spiersy's bit by now.

Jack starts laughing hard at something on his phone.

'No way,' he says between laughs. He glances up at Ellie before returning his attention back to his phone. 'That's a belter. He'll think twice before picking on you again.'

'Jack,' Sandra says. 'What have you done?'

'*Me?* Nothing at all.' He looks at Ellie, smiles and shakes his head before standing and heading for the door. 'I'm away round to Aiden's.'

I lock eyes with Sandra before we both turn our attention to our daughter.

'Ellie Angela McKinnon,' Sandra says, leaning forward. 'Is there something you want to tell us?'

'No Mummy,' she says as sweetly as only little girls know how.

'Are you sure?'

Ellie nods. 'Yes Mummy.'

Sandra's not buying it. She narrows her eyes and tilts her head at Ellie, but our little angel's unflustered.

Sandra sits back and sighs. 'Okay then.'

Ellie picks up her tablet and begins scrolling as my jaw near hits the table. She's glaring at the screen with a look on her face I can only describe as saying, 'Come ahead.'

I glance towards the heavens and smile. How the battlegrounds in the war against bullies have changed.

ROBBING THE HOOD

Robin took a deep breath as he finished filling the deep hole he had dug deep within Sherwood Forest. He hid the mound with branches until satisfied no one would notice the depths to which his betrayal sank. Creeping back from whence he came, he swept any sign of his tracks with a holly-bush branch before making for the clearing. By God and all things holy, he prayed the birds beginning to sing would remain silent on the whereabouts of his secret.

Before he had even snuck within long-bow-range of his camp, the joyful dawn-chorus was drowned out by a greater hum of joy – his band of merry men preparing for the day ahead.

Only, it was no longer a mere band. Or just men. His proclamation of robbing the rich to give to the poor had attracted man and maiden alike. From all corners of this island. From the sheer white-cliffs to the valleys of unpronounceable names. From the flea-infested city-slums to the mountain tops of the wild north. There were even those among them who spoke not a single word of God's English. Ravenous they came, united under the common language of making the rich pay. Delivered they were, by tall ships stocked with booty destined for the noblest in the realm. The same booty they came to liberate from said nobles.

By God, his merry band bore more likeness to an army. A host to rival the numbers fielded by *any* monarch in God's kingdoms. A horde united behind one cause – vengeance.

A snapping twig in the thick undergrowth behind caused him to stop and unsling his bow. His hand reached for his quiver as he took a knee facing the direction of the sound.

'My noblest sire of Loxley,' came a familiar voice from the shadows. 'How would the good Lord look upon thee at the end of days if you slayed his most worthy servant.'

Robin breathed a sigh of relief as his accomplice stepped out from the foliage.

Friar Tuck lowered his hood and slid his hands into the opposing sleeves of his robe – the fading moon cast an otherworldly glow atop his bald head. His long, brown garment looked more kin to a sack one would hawk potatoes in rather than clothing. The friar wore it not because he couldn't afford finer attire – the silk undergarment hidden 'neath his tunic attesting to this – but to present a mask of piety. His soft, rotund face betrayed the truth that any piety Friar Tuck had, was of the meat filled kind, and had been shovelled down his gullet.

'Is it done?' Friar Tuck asked.

'Aye.' Robin stood and slung his bow over his shoulder. 'It be done.'

'*Yes,* it *is* done.' The friar sighed and shook his head. 'I fear living this long among savages has made you uncouth. Never lose anchorage to your place in this world, *Sir* Robin.'

Robin scowled. 'It be done, it is done, what does it matter how I say it? It translates the same – betrayal.' Robin howked a piece of phlegm from his throat and spat it at his feet.

Friar Tuck recoiled. '*Why,* does it matter.'

'Why does what matter?'

'No, no, no,' Friar tuck said, waving his hands dismissively. 'It is not "what does it matter", as you uttered, but *why* does it matter.'

Robin turned and made his way to camp before saying something he might regret.

'Wait!' called Friar Tuck. 'We must align our story before presenting it to the masses.'

'Our story! More like our lies.'

Friar Tuck caught up with Robin, clearly out of breath. 'Hush, Sir Robin, lest the peasants hear us.'

'What does it matter? They'll hear soon enough.'

'*Why*, does—'

Robin stopped and turned to face the friar. His hand darted to his pommel. 'By God, if you correct me one more time, I'll cut that robe from your back and parade you in front of the peasants in your silk undergarments.'

Friar Tuck's face dropped, his bottom lip quivering. 'My dear, dear Robin. I mean no offence. I merely wish you to retain some semblance of decorum and nobility lest the great lords and ladies might look down upon thee when all is said and done.'

'The only factor in how the great lords and ladies might look upon me depends on whether I be successful in putting this rabble back in their cage.'

'True, and that is why we simply *must* make sure we convince them.'

Robin glanced to the heavens as he kneaded a knot in the back of his neck. 'How then, noblest servant of God, do we manage that improbable task?'

'We must persuade them that it is in their best interest. And if that fails—'

'Which it will.'

'—and if that fails, we shall strike the fear of God into their hearts.'

'Literally?'

'Very much so,' the Friar said with a devious smirk. 'It is one of the many, many, perquisites of the job.'

'I remain unconvinced we can do *anything* to rein them in. The barn door is wide ajar, and every horse, donkey and ass hath fled the yoke.'

'Perhaps.' Friar Tuck stroked his chin and nodded. 'Or perhaps not. The noblest among us know there are but two ways to make an ass do as you command. You might dangle a carrot in front of its greedy snout, and it shall bear the most oppressive of burdens in the effort of capturing it. The only problem being that sometimes it manages to snatch the carrot. But alas, I fear the carrot method is precisely what has led us into the mire we find ourselves in.'

'Not a truer word a friar has uttered yet. Although, that is hardly a difficult accomplishment to achieve.'

The insult created a look of incredulity etched across the friar's face. Even though it gave Robin his first taste of joy in a long time, he showed all the emotion of a blacksmith's hammer at the jibe.

Friar Tuck crossed himself, clasped his hands together, and gazed to the heavens. 'Dear Lord, King of Kings, Protector of the Meek, source of all that is good, please forgive your son, Robin of Loxley, for his transgressions. His mind and tongue have been poisoned by the unwashed masses. Those uncouth ones that eat with the same hand with which they wipe excrement from their behinds. Bear witness that I take his sin as my own, and if the good lord sees fit, strike me down now instead of the simple Robin Hood.' The friar closed his eyes and muttered a latinate prayer.

Robin ignored the pretense of moral superiority. 'What be the second method for driving asses?'

The friar opened his eyes slowly, feigning surprise that he still stood unsmote. 'Alas, dear Robin, it seems I have done thee yet another favour with the good Lord.'

'Thank you, oh pious one, your generosity knows no bounds. Although as sure as an arrow flies from my bow, I wager those debts will be paid in kind.'

The friar could barely contain his smirk. 'That, I have no doubt. Now, where was I?'

'Second way to control—'

'Ah, yes, yes. The only other way, and perhaps the surest, is to use the stick. And it just so happens'—he slipped a hand deep inside his robe and pulled a leather bound bible from it—'I have the biggest stick in Sherwood Forest.'

'God's word?'

The friar smirked. 'More than that. God's will. Come. Daybreak is upon us. We must capture them before they set out. I shall do the talking.' The friar headed off in the direction of their camp.

Robin released a deep sigh. 'I am sure you will.' He hastily followed the Friar. 'It be the only thing I am sure of.'

Following the friar like a sheepdog behind its master, Robin skulked through the mass of folk commonly known as his merry men. And merry they were on this brisk, summer morn. Every smile, curtsy, bow, and firm back slap made his heart sink lower and lower so that he became convinced it would fall from his leggings and be snatched to the fiery depths below. By the time he reached the triad of fires with the large iron-pots suspended over them, the sun's first rays penetrated the forest canopy. The heat from the cooking fires and sun in stark contrast to the coldness within.

A man in ragged clothes dropped his own bowl and filled another from one of the pots. He almost tripped in his haste to bring it to Robin. The downhearted look that consumed the man's face when Robin waved him away was kin to kicking a puppy.

Friar Tuck cleared his throat. 'Come ye, hear ye, one and all. The Lord has spoken and entrusted I with his will.'

Mumbled groans answered the friar, as was always the case with morning prayers. Robin's band had better things to do. Like liberating shiny rings from fat, grubby fingers. He shuddered at the thought that the only prayers occurring this morning would be silent ones uttered by himself.

A bead of sweat streamed down the inside of his arm as the folk gathered around him and the friar like a giant noose. Dozens deep they stood – ragged, dirt-caked, and barely a full set of teeth among them. Yet not a single one wore a frown.

'I pray the Lord blesses us wi' a speedy prayer this fine morn,' someone in the crowd called. 'Gives us meek folk more time t' claim wer charity.'

Robin tugged at his collar as the crowd chuckled.

'Hold that tongue,' Friar Tuck commanded. 'Lest it be taken by the Devil and put to nefarious tasks.'

'D'ya hear that, Marion?' the same man called again. 'Could be your lucky night.'

The crowd broke into belly laughs.

The friar, looking flustered, crossed himself before roaring, 'Silence! The Lord does *not* tolerate this decadent language, especially before his most humble of servants. Perhaps this sort of wanton sinful behaviour is exactly why he has commanded so.'

'Commanded so wot?' another voice called.

'The good Lord,' continued the friar, 'in all his infinite wisdom, begs you cease with your immoral ways.'

'Ah now, good Friar, ye'll have t' be more specific t' which immoral ways ye speak o', as there're sins committed here wot are no even in that fancy book o' yours.'

'Aye,' came a voice from the back of the crowd. 'But that's wit makes this sae gid a place tae bide!'

The crowd roared in laughter once more.

Friar Tuck looked at Robin in a silent request for assistance.

Robin forced a smile upon his face and raised his hands. He shouted above the din, 'Please, good folk, lend the friar your ears.'

'He may take young Will's,' a tall man at the front said, pushing another who stood beside him forward. 'He has enough for us all!'

Young Will punched his tormentor on the arm before stepping back into the crowd under a hail of laughter and derision – his massive ears beaming red.

Robin allowed the faux smile to flee from his face as he looked the jester in the eye. He placed a hand out, palm up, and said, 'Apple,' all the while keeping his intent gaze fixed upon the tall man.

The crowd fell silent. A young maiden stepped forward and placed an apple onto Robin's palm.

Robin tossed the apple high in the direction of the man he glared at.

As quick as a hare with a fox on its tail, Robin unslung his bow, cocked an arrow in it, and took aim at the man.

There was a collective intake of breath as Robin loosed the arrow. It struck the apple a mere hand above the tall man's head, covering him in mashed apple, and soaring above the crowd and into a tree behind them.

Robin casually slung his bow across his back. 'Any more jesters have any more jesting to do?'

No answer came.

'Thank you,' Robin said. 'Friar Tuck, please continue.'

'Splendid folk of Sherwood Forest,' said Friar Tuck. 'The all knowing God in his infinite wisdom sent his servant, Saint Jude, to I in a vision as I prayed for your souls this morning. Saint Jude was *not* pleased.' The Friar crossed himself and kissed his finger. 'In this vision, Saint Jude did reveal to *I*, the folly of *your* ways. He showed you good people, weighed down by your ill-gotten gains, unable to ascend to the kingdom of heaven.'

A number of the crowd clutched their hearts and gasped. Most bore a look of tired cynicism.

The friar was a master at spinning a yarn, but it seemed he had his work cut out here.

He continued his narrative. 'Alas, I fear your gratuitous plundering has ushered thee into the dominion of none other than Lucifer himself. For the good Saint Jude did show me the final battle, and shamefully, this band of merry men before me were *not* on the side of good. Rather, you'—the friar pointed at random folk in the crowd—'you, you, ALL of you gathered here, were in the vanguard of the horde of darkness.' The friar bowed his head – a mask of pity and shame etched across his face.

This seemed to shock more of the crowd as a number of them crossed themselves and uttered prayers of forgiveness. Robin's shoulders relaxed at the crowd's reaction. It seemed enough of them were being swayed.

'But Friar,' a maiden's voice called from the crowd. 'Wot o' your original vision o' Saint Vincent de Paul? You know, the one wot the greedy farmer was hoarding all the grain.'

The friar's head remained bowed, but his eyes darted around. Robin willed him not to lose the impetus now.

After what seemed an eternally long pause, the friar lifted his head. 'Alas, the good Saint Jude did reveal to I, that none other than Lucifer himself tricked me. It was *he* who presented himself to I in my original vision, donned in the likeness of Saint Vincent de Paul. Shamefully, I fell for the ruse, and for that sin, I offer up my eternal penance.' The friar covered his face with both hands and shook his head.

If the religion racket ever dries up the friar would surely flourish on the theatrical stage.

'But,' said the maiden. 'How can you be sure the vision wot you had this morn weren't Lucifer, donned in the likeness of Saint Jude, and the first vision wos actually Saint Vincent de Paul?'

The friar froze, his mouth ajar.

Robin held his breath, willing the friar to come up with a plausible reason.

'Aye,' said a man in the crowd. 'That seems t' me t' be the sort o' double-crossin scheme wot Lucifer might try.'

More dissenting voices joined the two. The friar was losing them.

'Because, dear friends,' he finally said, 'after this morning's dire caution, I did witness Saint Jude ascend towards the heavens above.'

'Towards?' someone else called from the crowd. 'Did ye see um actually *enter* the Kingdom o' Heaven?'

'Well, of course not.'

'Then how can ye be sure it wasna Lucifer and he just made it look like he were ascending t' heaven. For all we know, as soon as he wos out o' sight, he could've descended back t' hell.'

'No, no, no,' said Friar Tuck. 'That is unlikely the case.'

'Unlikely, but no impossible.'

Robin willed the friar to quell the swell of support shifting in favour of the dissenters.

'Robin,' one of them called. 'Wot does you say?'

Robin's heart quickened under the scrutiny of the entire crowd. He opened his dry mouth, but no words came out.

The friar – squirming and looking uncomfortable – said, 'No, no, good folk, thou are misguided. You simply *must* trust I. It is only through I that thee shall escape eternal damnation.'

'Ah c'mon now, Friar. Ye'll be walkin on water next.'

'Aye, an turnin bread intae pies!'

'Well, as sure as flies flock t' shit, I'll no be endin me charity raids at the word o' a friar wot's just admitted he wos tricked by Lucifer.'

'Never before,' Friar Tuck said, slow and deliberate, 'have I bore witness to such blasphemy.' He shook his head. 'I am but a mere messenger for God's will. Ignore the warning at your own peril. Mark my words – continue with your nefarious ways and the good Lord will have no option but to cast you out.'

It seemed to Robin, this attempt of stoking the fear of God into the people was falling on deaf ears.

'Nae,' someone called. 'I'm no buyin it.'

'Aye, me neither. It all seems patchy tae me. And wit aboot they Moors fae the land o' eternal sand dunes? They dinna even pray tae the same God as the Friar.'

'Aye, it's some fella called Alan.'

'It's Allah, ya eejit.'

'Potatoe, potahto. Must they lads cease their ways?'

'As theirs is a false religion under a false god,' said the friar, 'they are already damned.'

'But must they follow the will o' your God?'

'Well...no, not if—'

'It's simple then. We should all start prayin tae this Alan. Here, someone try t' find oot wit their heaven be like.'

'I hear they get seventy-two virgins.'

'Where do they get them from 'cause it sure as hell aint from this camp.'

'Could be all the friar's, priests and nuns!'

'God, can ye imagine?'

'That sounds like hell t' me. Give me two fire-breathin whores from the slums any day.'

'Aye, but that's only if ye believe the holy ones when they say they've never bedded a maiden.'

Robin and Friar Tuck shared a bewildered glance. Not only must they convince the mob to cease their merry ways, they were now about to lose their flock to another religion.

'What now?' whispered Robin.

The Friar raised his brow, a look of shock and helplessness across his face.

'HOLD IT!' bellowed a familiar voice from within the masses.

All eyes turned in the direction of the command.

Robin had never been so relieved to see Little John's beard-covered face, protruding above most others as he pushed through the crowd.

Little John had a habit of digging Robin out of the dung, but as the big man broke from the ranks carrying the muddy sack and chest, any hope Robin had of his old pal rescuing him quickly vanished.

He marched up to Robin and dropped the chest at his feet with a thud. Little John's dark eyes bore right into Robin's.

'Did ye lose somethin, *Sir* Robin?' he growled, his words like a dagger.

'You followed me?' Robin whispered.

'Only for protection. I've had my suspicions that our ranks have been infiltrated by those who would do us harm. I wanted t' make sure you were safe when ye wandered off on your own. Never would I have believed, that the snake in our garden would be our dear, glorious leader himself.'

'Please, good friend, I beg of you, do not —'

'*Friend*,' snorted Little John. He drew his eyes from Robin and untied the rope holding the sack closed. '*Friends* do not betray one another.'

'For the love of God, I beg of you. Come with me and we shall discuss the matter in private.'

'Anything you must say shall be said for one and all t' hear.' Little John reached into the sack.

'John,' hissed Friar Tuck. 'It need not be done this wa—'

'Silence that treasonous, lying tongue!' roared Little John. He reached into the sack and turned to the crowd. 'It appears our wise and noble leaders have a secret. A secret they tried t' bury from us. Literally. I present t' one and all, evidence o' their betrayal.' He reached into the sack, pulled the contents from it, and held them up before the masses.

Robin's world collapsed to the sound of horrified gasps from the crowd. The shock Friar Tuck had so desperately tried to instill in the people presented itself at John's terrible revelation.

One of them called out, 'Surely no. Is that...?'

'Sir Robin o' Loxley,' Little John said. 'Proudly posing for a portrait with none other than Sir Geoffrey Epstone o' the Fair Maiden Isle.'

Robin wiped a sleeve across his sodden brow. 'But friends, please understand. That was *before* everyone knew of his...misdeeds.'

'Does "before everyone knew" include you?' Little John said.

Robin swallowed hard as the initial shock of the crowd turned to anger.

'Who be that in the background?' one of them called.

'That, my good men and fair maidens,' Little John said, 'be the pious Friar Tuck, frolicking with some young maiden.' Friar Tuck opened his mouth but Little John raised a hand to silence him. 'No doubt the *good* Friar will try t' pass it off as him relieving her o' her sins.'

'Wot o' the chest?' someone called.

'Ahh,' Little John said, handing the painting to someone in the crowd. He undid the latch to the leather-bound chest, and placed a bear-like hand upon the lid. 'This be their prize for selling us good folk out.' He lifted the lid, revealing to one and all, Robin and Friar Tuck's ill-gotten gains.

The crowd stood open-mouthed and silent at the mound of shiny coins in the chest. Little John scooped a handful and let them trickle through his fingers back into the chest.

A maiden standing at the front asked, 'Where did all them come from?'

'Them,' said Little John, 'come from a deep hole, deep within the heart of Sherwood Forest. A hole I witnessed being dug this very morn by our glorious leader.'

The maiden turned her cold, hard gaze to Robin. 'And where did *he* get all them from?'

'Shall we ask him?' Little John said.

The crowd spoke in agreement as Robin wished Satan would open a hole in the ground and be done with him.

Little John turned to Robin. 'Well...?'

Robin swallowed hard. 'Please, good folk, allow me to—'

'Speak up, traitor,' someone called from the back of the crowd. 'Lies don't carry well on this wind.'

Robin sighed and bowed his head. 'No more lies will cross these lips.'

'Robin,' said Friar Tuck, his words like an arrow of ice. 'Do not be so fooli—'

'Enough!' commanded Robin. 'The people deserve the truth.' Robin lifted his head and looked at those stood before him. Their once admiration-filled eyes replaced by loathing and contempt. 'It be as Little John tells – I have betrayed you all.'

'But why, Robin?' a young boy asked.

'Greed, shame, lack of a spine,' said Robin. 'Take your pick. The facts be I took these coins in exchange for dissuading your good selves from raiding the wealthy.'

'I no understand, why would you want t' do so?'

'Do not be so green, boy,' a stout man said. 'The great Robin o' Loxley didna *want* t' sell us out for a chest o' coins. He *had* t' do so, lest his transgressions with Geoffrey Epstone be known t' one and all.'

'And wot o' Friar Tuck?' a maiden asked. 'Was that why the *good* friar were so resolute in his tale o' Saint Jude?'

'I cannot speak for the friar,' Robin said. 'As much as the friar cannot speak for Saint Jude.' Robin looked Friar Tuck in the eyes and raised his brow.

The friar, looking panicked with his bottom lip quivering, said, 'I can assure you all, as God is my witness, I had NO part in this treacher—'

The people had stomached enough and broke into hails of derision. Some tossed putrid fruit his way.

'Please,' begged the friar, flapping like a moth on a web. 'How would the good Lord look upon thee—'

'Be silent, *Friar*,' Little John said. 'Keep your manipulative words for your maker.'

'Aye! Let's send them t' their maker.'

'Aye, hang em high so's they don't have far t' travel.'

'I'll get t' rope.'

'No!' called Little John. 'Wait! Do not kill them.'

'How no?'

'Because we are not murderers.'

'They deserve nothin less.'

'Indeed, but think o' the consequences. If we kill these fools it'll give every king, baron, and bishop the perfect excuse t' demonise us as the dogs they view us t' be, and hunt us all down. Do not let our anger be used as a tool for them t' divide us even more from their tall towers.'

'But they must pay.'

'Aye,' said Little John. 'That, they must.'

'Yet you speak in their defence? Why *are* ye so keen t' let them off the hook?'

Someone gasped, 'He be in cahoots.'

'Aye, it must be so.'

'Get him!'

Little John unsheathed his great axe, swung it an overhead arc, and crashed it into the chest of coins. 'Cease this madness! I am neither one of them nor do I believe they should get off Scot-free.'

'Bloody racist,' a red-haired man muttered.

'How would you have them punished then?' another asked.

A devious smile crept across Little John's face. 'Get me the lamest ass we have, a branch from the yew tree, a length of rope, and a carrot.'

* * *

Robin's eyes watered from the putrid onion gagged in his mouth. The thick rope binding his hands together chafed at his wrist, and his naked skin – covered in rotten food – prickled in the early-morning breeze. Only his back retained some degree of heat thanks to the naked Friar Tuck bound upon the ass behind him.

With every lumbering step the ass took towards the carrot strung upon a piece of yew branch before them, Robin's shame grew tenfold. He knew *precisely* where the road his band of merry men had set them upon led. He couldn't help but imagine the derision the people of Nottingham would greet them with, when the three asses lumbered through the town's great gate. He could already hear the ridicule and mockery in store for them from the town's sheriff.

The ass heehawed and snatched at the carrot as it crested a hill.

Robin hung his head in shame as the walls of the great town came into view.

COME FLY WITH ME

The youtubers make it look easy-peasy but I can *never* do it. You need to make a *biiiig* cross – not the Jesus one but the same one as the white cross on our flag – just like this. Put one end frew the bottom of the cross and pull tight. That's the easy part. Next you need to make a bunny ear wif one lace and then make a bunny ear wif the other lace, but how can you make the second bunny ear wif only one hand? Oh well, at least airyplanes don't need to know how to tie shoe laces...because they don't have any feet! Do you know what airyplanes go like?

They go, 'Neeeaaaaahhhw...neeeaaaaahhhw.'

That's what the big airyplanes go like when they fly away from the airyport and go right over my house. I've seen loads and loads today – more than ten. Do you know I can count all the way up to fifty by myself? Wifout even using my fingers? My teacher, Mzzz Campbell, told me I was very clever to count all the way to fifty on my own. I like Mzzz Campbell. She's got a nice smile and nice hair and wears pretty clothes just like a princess. When I first went to the big school, not the big BIG school, but the big primary-school one, I was *so* scared and I didn't want to let go of Magda's hand but Mzzz Campbell came over and asked me my name and when I told her it was Hope she smiled and said, 'I hope Hope will be a brave big girl and come into school with me.' Magda laughed and so did I even though I never even knowed what the joke was but I just liked to hear my name twice and Mzzz Campbel smiled and held out her hand and I took it and we went inside. I did feel a little bit sad for Magda because she wouldn't have anyone to listen to her silly songs when she did the washing and ironing and hoovering because mummy is never *ever* back from work before it gets dark. Sometimes mummy has to live in another house for a few days when her boss, who I fink is called Eddie Tor, needs her to go and tell people about all the bad fings that are happening far away. Magda stays over these times and watches me and we have ice-cream and sweeties and she lets me watch anyfing I want. Sometimes if I'm really really sad and mummy has been away for ages and ages and I'm really missing her Magda will let me watch mummy on the news but never wif the volume up so I can't hear what mummy is saying. I sometimes watch her lips and make up what she is saying in my head. Fings like, 'My little girl Hope is the bestest little girl in the world,' and 'I love my little Hope *sooo* much.' But then the news goes to the bits wif people fighting or cars on fire or people crying and Magda says, 'That's enough,' in her funny little voice that sounds just like the meerkats on the adverts and turns it over.

Neeeeeeaaaahhhhhhww

I look up at the big white airyplane wif the red stripe and red tail and wave at the people on the airyplane. I hope they can see me sitting up here on the roof and I inmaga...inmaging...inmagination they are all waving back and smiling and saying, 'There's Hope, the bestest airyplane noise-maker in the whole wide world.' Did you like my airyplane noise? Close your eyes and I'll do it again. Pretend you don't know I'm trying to do a airyplane noise. Okay, are you ready? Here comes my inpression, tell me what you fink it is.

'Neeeeeaaaaahhhhhww...neeeeeaaaaahhhw.'

Did you guess it was a airyplane? I hope so because if you know what it is then my mummy will know what it is when she comes home and she will be *so* proud of her little Hope. Mzzz Campbell knowed what it is today at school when I asked her to guess what I was. You know what, I didn't even have to climb to the top of the climbing frame and show her me flying, I just made the airyplane noise and she said, 'You can be anything you want to be, Hope.' That's what she said to Sophia when she said she didn't identiti...identitif...iden...want to be a little girl anymore. Mzzz Campbell hugged her and gave her a special badge wif her—no, *his* new name on it and said Jack is a brave little boy and we should all be happy and nice to him and Mzzz Campbell told us all to clap and cheer and Jack looked *soooo* happy standing at the front of the class wif everyone saying his new name. I was *sooo* happy for Jack and I wished I'd fought of the idea first but then I remembered I wouldn't like being a boy because boys are mean and stinky and they like to fight and fart but at least Jack can still use the girls toilet as I fink he needs to wait till he grows a winky. I tried finking for ages and ages what I could be that would make me so happy like Jack and have my mummy and everyone smiling and saying my name.

'Hope! It is not funny anymore.'

Uh-oh, Magda is back out the front looking for me. Mrs Walker from the seventh floor right below my house is wif her. She's saying, 'Please, Hope, come out from wherever you are. You won't be in any trouble if you come out now.'

I move back a tiny bit and hold my breath and keep as quiet as a mouse. Then I hear a car stop and I peek over the edge and see mummy getting out her car and Magda run up to her. I jump up like a happy kangaroo.

'Look, mummy! Guess what I am now!'

I run along the small flat bit right at the top of the roof wif my arms out wide.

'Neeeeeeeaaaahhhhhhhww!'

I reach the end and stop and turn.

'Neeeeaaaahhw...I'm a airyplane no—'

Uh-oh! I forgoted real airyplanes don't have feet when I trip on my shoe lace and fall onto the steep bit of the roof and slide down towards the edge...

'HOOOOPE!'

...and now I'm flying like a bird, a bee, a REAL big airyplane. Flying fast down past my house, past Mrs Walker's house, while going, 'Neeeaahw,' and my mummy, MY mummy, she's shouting my name, MY name, and running towards me wif her arms open wide. Just like a airyplane.

STREAM OF TRANQUILLITY

Tommy never saw the bullet that punched a hole in his head, blew his broken brain apart, and ended his torment. He knew his killer.

The day began like most others that summer. Gaunt and haggard young men huddled around wooden ladders while shells whistled overhead. The shelling was among the more tranquil moments. When the shells rained, there was no fighting.

Tommy – a brawler all his life – never imagined he'd grow weary of scrapping. That was before his life had descended into an endless onslaught of never-ending battles.

He fought the cold and damp, the lice and bloated corpse-rats. He resisted sleep and the ensuing nightmares. He wrestled with the appalling visions haunting his mind. Dreadful visions of atrocities he'd seen, and shamefully, committed. He resisted the desire to speak with the pals he'd enlisted with. Looking into their bleary-eyes was like peering into a mirror. A cracked, warped mirror on the verge of breaking into a thousand pieces. He grappled to keep the creeping shadow of sorrow from consuming him each and every day. Sorrow for the pals who'd never fight again. He fought to keep hidden, the petrifying anxiousness now entrenched in his very being.

All this before a different whistle commanded him to face his most formidable foe.

Tommy tensed as the big guns behind fell silent. He glanced over his shoulder.

Lieutenant Evans focused on his pocket watch as he placed his ACME whistle between pursed lips. He would utter no inspiring words to encourage his men to a gallant victory. He reached for the only motivator he knew – his prized, captured Luger.

Tommy turned and focused on the battered tin hat in front. He shuffled on swollen, numb feet. Sweat trickled down the inside of his arm, and he would've vomited if his stomach hadn't been empty. He begged and prayed to a god he'd long lost all faith in.

Lieutenant Evans' whistle joined the chorus blasting along the line. Raking gunfire, exploding grenades, and ear-shattering artillery answered.

Tommy's vision narrowed on the tin hat in front as his world descended into chaos. Shrieking whistles, shouts and screams, gunfire and explosions all dissolved around him. It was surreal, like a dream, or more likely, a dreadful nightmare.

The tin hat in front became a man's back, arse, legs and boots, until all before him was a mud-caked ladder.

Tommy stepped onto the ladder as a deafening blast reverberated above. Debris rained down. Amid clods of earth, the disappeared boots and legs crashed on top of him, sending him sprawling backwards. He scrambled to his knees, straightened his tin hat, and froze. The boots and legs were missing an arse, back, and tin hat.

Terror descended upon him, pushing and squeezing the life from him. Chest tight with fear, he struggled to breathe and wanted to tear the clothes from his back. His trembling fingers loosened the helmet strap from his throat as rough hands pulled him to his feet.

'Get up that fucking ladder!' Lieutenant Evans roared, pushing Tommy against it. 'NOW!'

Tommy shook his head. He opened his mouth but no words came out. He panted in a vain attempt to get more oxygen into his lungs.

Lieutenant Evans skelped the back of his head, sending his tin hat flying. He flung Tommy against the trench wall. Cold, damp earth filled one ear, as warm, wet breath filled the other.

'Get your arse in gear. Get it up that there ladder. And join your brothers.' The lieutenant pressed his Luger against Tommy's temple. 'Do not test me, boy.'

Tommy's legs buckled and he collapsed to his knees. 'Please, Boss, please,' he sobbed. 'I can't do it no more, I can't. Please don't make me.'

The lieutenant cocked his pistol.

Tommy's eyes fell upon his own battered and beaten tin hat as he bowed his head. 'I'm sorry. Tell my—'

Tommy knew his killer. Lieutenant Evans' shrill cry of 'COWARD!' was the last word anyone spoke to him.

A BREATH OF FRESH AIR

I'm gripping the steering wheel tight as I swerve around the congested hogmanay traffic.

'Looks like a job,' Lizzy comments from behind.

Curiosity beats me and I steal a glance towards the housing scheme. A black smoke-plume rises with menace into the clear, midday sky.

A breathless voice crackles over the radio. 'Message for oncoming crew – two BA wearers required as soon as you roll up.'

Shit. My right foot responds by pressing the accelerator harder, even though it's already jammed against the floor.

'Roger,' says the gaffer into the mic. He turns to my three colleagues in the back. 'Right guys, no dicking about, get into air.'

The distinctive whoosh of air and bleeps from the breathing-apparatus sets starting up fills the cab. There's no other sound – no other command. Everyone knows what needs to be done.

Our pace slows to a frustrating crawl as we turn into the housing scheme and weave past haphazardly parked cars.

'Arseholes,' Lizzy rightly points out.

No one gives a second thought when abandoning their car. What if a large vehicle needs to pass? What if that large vehicle is a fire engine? What if that fire engine is responding to a house on fire? What if that house on fire is home to a loved one of *yours*?

We eventually turn onto the street. It's alive with people waving and

45

pointing us towards the burning building with the big, red fire-engine outside. Cheers folks, don't know how we'd have found it without yous. Some of them even have the cheek to film the spectacle on their phones. It's good to see someone's misery can be turned into a positive – by getting likes on social media. Honestly, you couldn't give some folk a red face with a blowtorch.

We rock up behind the first engine, and the doors open before we come to a stop. I jump out, sprint to the first engine, and unfurl its second hose-reel. Lizzy assists while Davey and Grant – donned in breathing apparatus – make for the house.

We drag the hose to them as the gaffer from the first crew in attendance finishes giving them their brief. '...unsure if there's anyone inside, so I need yous to search and rescue.'

Acrid smoke looking like cauliflower heads pulses from the half-open front door.

Jesus. I pray there *isn't* anyone inside.

Davey and Grant grab the hose-reel, and march through the garden towards the smoke-filled doorway. Me and Lizzy follow, dragging the hose and laying it out in zig-zags across the garden. Just as they're about to step inside, my worst fear comes true. The first BA team appears from the smoke-filled doorway like Matthew Kelly's just called, 'Come on down!' A small, lifeless body cradled in one of their arms.

I grab her from them and turn. 'Get me the trauma kit!'

I run to the bottom of the garden with her listless body slumped across my arms. Her golden hair is stained black with soot, and her blank eyes are half closed. Her tongue lolls from her slack jaw, and she looks not to be breathing.

Please don't be dead.

I gently lay her on the grass. 'What's the ETA for the ambulance?'

'I'll find out,' the gaffer says.

Lizzy joins me with the trauma kit. She tears it open as I check the casualty. I place an ear at her mouth, a hand over her chest, and hold my breath.

'Anything?' Lizzy asks, the hope clear in her voice.

I nearly punch the air when the faintest whisper of breath caresses my cheek, and a racing heartbeat prods my hand.

'She's alive,' I cry like Dr Frankenstein.

'Is she breathing?'

'Barely, but her heart's going ten-to-the-dozen,' I say, praying it's a strong heart beating within this young one.

'Oxygen ready,' Lizzy says.

I slip the strap over her head, and fix the mask around her nose and mouth. 'Okay, turn it on, top setting, she's going to need it.'

After a slight whoosh of air, the reservoir bag on her face-mask fills with life-giving oxygen. I will her to give me a sign, something, *anything*, that she's going to make it.

She obliges, but it's not what I want to see. Her eyes roll back in her skull, and her limbs tense and shoot straight out.

'Oh-no,' Lizzy says.

'Where's that fucking ambulance!' I roar.

'On it's way,' says the gaffer.

'When will it be here?'

'It'll be here when it's here. Until then, it's up to us. Now stop bitching and do what you can.'

'C'mon pal,' I plea, stroking her head. 'Don't give up, keep fighting.'

'Keep away from that fucking light,' Lizzy says, her voice wavering.

The surrounding chaos fades as I focus on the young casualty fighting for her life on the damp grass before me. The longer she flirts with the angel of death, the more likely she'll stay in the otherworld.

Lizzy – as tough a bird as you'll ever meet – looks like she's about to cry. I know *exactly* how she feels.

I wipe my sweaty brow with the arm of my tunic. This feeling of helplessness is stifling. No one deserves to go out like this. But someone so young with their whole life ahead? Well, unfair doesn't even *begin* to touch it.

'Look!' Lizzy says. 'She's coming around.'

I breathe a heavy sigh of relief when her limbs relax and her pupils come back into view.

This is good.

She settles into a normal breathing rhythm – I gladly do the same.

She blinks open her eyes and looks around. God knows what she's thinking seeing all this commotion in her garden, and me – smiling from ear to ear – staring into her eyes. They're all bloodshot and bleary, but at the same time, the most beautiful eyes I've ever had the pleasure to look into. They're full of life.

'You think she's going to make it?' Lizzy says.

I wasn't sure...until she gave me a sign that confirmed it. And, when that Golden Labrador puppy began wagging her tail, I knew she'd be just fine.

TODAY'S THE DAY

'Arrghhh! For *fuck* sake.'

There's another couple hundred quid down the drain.

A salty metallic flavour rouses my tongue as I suck on my bloodied knuckle. An unfamiliar face glares at me from the darkened and – thanks to they simple-minded cunts – now cracked laptop screen. Could be a picture of dad I'm looking at, with the paler than healthy complexion, hollowed cheeks, bloodhound eyes, and thinning hair.

Do I really look that old?

I close my eyes and for the briefest of moments, I swear, the pungent and aromatic scents from his cigars wafts up my nose.

'You're only as old as the lassie you're feeling,' he used to say.

What if you're no feeling any girl, *dad*, and hadn't for the past two years? And what if two years is the lie you tell everyone – and yourself – so's they don't think you're a complete and utter waster?

I shake my head and slam the laptop shut before it gets bounced off the wall. I push myself from the tattered leather-recliner that's become my bed. After a couple of joints, walking the whole ten paces to my bedroom feels like a quest no even Harold and Kumar would attempt. More and more afternoons I wake there with joypad in hand, telly on standby, and last night's leftover munchies on the fold-away table next to me.

At least I'm never stuck for breakfast.

49

This morning, I mean afternoon, I woke to find a half-empty bag of Maltesers, and an unopened bag of Doritos. Looked like it was going to be a good day. Until I fired up the computer. Barely watched two videos of the latest shite these cretins were spewing before it was onto all my social media accounts.

Somebody's got to tell them how wrong they are, right?

That's when the proverbial shit hit the fan. But then again, it always does. Why can't they see how fucked up their retarded opinions are?

'Son, opinions are like arseholes,' dad used to say. 'Everybody has one, and some of them stink.'

Speaking of stinking, I'll need to get they bed sheets cleaned. The spunk stains from the last time I managed the perilous voyage to the old wanking chariot will have grown arms and legs by now. I peer through my bedroom door, trying to remember the last night I spent there. Could've been a few weeks ago. Wouldn't be surprised if it was months.

'Ahh, fuck it,' I say to the only person I seem to talk to these days. 'I'll do it the morra.'

I close my bedroom door, feeling that way when you're balls-deep on an acid trip, and your absolutely certain you've done this before. I wander into the kitchen and turn on the hot tap, even though I know I'll no get any hot water from it. The gas bill is way down my list of debts. Probably because they won't kick the shit out of me for not paying. And given the choice between cold showers or having Malky Cunninghame and his team of heavies booting your door in, what would you choose?

Exactly.

You've likely heard the same as me anyway – that your hair and skin cleans itself naturally if you leave it long enough. We probably bathe ourselves too much these days anyway. At the very least, I'm doing my bit to help fight global warming, no?

Bloodied water trickles over the mountain of dishes and pools in a chipped mug. It's the same shade the toilet water goes when an unflushed tampon lurks from the down pipe like some kinda underwater mouse.

Fuck it. The tap's on. May as well make an attempt at these dishes. If I can get these done it might not be a totally wasted day.

'Don't put off till the morra what can be done the day,' is another thing dad used to say.

Wise words.

I could really use some of his wisdom now. Every day I sink deeper and deeper into this funk. Like in the old westerns he loved watching. When a cowboy stumbles into some quicksand, and no matter what he does or how hard he tries, he only makes things worse.

How deep into this quagmire am I?

Feels like right up to my chin. Head tilted and motionless for fear of slipping beyond the point of no return. Hoping, begging, for someone to appear from the wilderness and throw me a line.

And I don't mean the kind you put up your nose. Although, I likely wouldn't knock it back. Probably a good idea to meet my maker with a bit of the old Columbian marching-powder propping me up. Swaggering up to the pearly gates like I own the fucking place. Sparking St Peter out before booting the gates clean off their hinges. Marching in there like John Wick, grabbing God by the throat and roaring, 'Hoi! Big man. What the *fuck* are you playing at?'

I notice I'm breathing deep when the rancid scent from the bin wafts up my nostrils. Think the water's had a soothing sort of meditative effect as without noticing, I'm down to the last of the cutlery at the bottom of the sink.

I shake my head and smile.

Why had this become such a big deal?

Maybe this is the day I'll be rescued from my pit. And maybe the person doing the rescuing will be me. That's double-bubble right there.

'Yep,' I say, nodding my head. 'Today's the day.'

I reach out and pull the cord on the blinds. Sunlight bathes the room and warms my skin.

There's the mother-fuckin energy I need.

As soon as I've finished these dishes, I'll empty that bin, fling my bed sheets in the washing, and jump in a shower. I don't even give a fuck that it'll be freezing. In fact, I'm actually looking forward to it. Standing there letting the cleansing water do its thing. I'm all giddy inside and my hands are shaking.

This is better than any cut-to-fuck intoxicant punted by Malky.

I grab the last dish – the big, rusting kitchen-knife. Might even go for a walk later. Can't remember the last time I was outside. Would be good to get some fresh air.

I glance up and out the window as I'm scrubbing the knife and it's like being kicked square in the balls.

There, in the park across the road from my flat, a father is running alongside his son, holding onto the seat of his tiny bike. He lets go and the wee boy continues along the path all on his own. The father jumps for joy.

Fuckin sickening.

I grit my teeth, desperately trying to keep the putrid bile scalding the back of my throat at bay. The most comforting thing dad used to say bounces around my head like a drunk on a trampoline. 'I'll always be there for you, pal.'

I shake my head clench my jaw. 'Fuckin liar.'

I glance at my trembling hands. The knife's hovering over my wrist. I look up, hoping to see the wee boy lying face down, crying for his dad.

He's still going. Pedalling furiously along his path away from his dad.

'Prick,' I mutter through pursed lips. 'Why did you have to leave me?' My vision blurs and I'm sobbing like a wean.

The sharp blade and cold water against my wrist are both terrifying and welcoming.

Looks like this is the only route out of hell.

I take one last deep breath.

The moment before I open my wrist, movement in the park catches my eye.

It's *them.*

Sauntering through the green space like they own the fuckin place. Three of the clowns I'd argued with so often online. Well, likely no *exactly* them, but judging by their appearance, they're the same types.

My blurred vision is replaced by a misty red one. Raw, animalistic rage builds inside. It's like being on a train track with a runaway train approaching. A distant rumble, slowly building into an earth-shaking roar by the moment.

Who the *fuck* do they think they are?

I'm gripping the handle of the knife tight as my train derails. My vision narrows on these *cunts.*

I'll show them.

I turn the tap off and head for the door.

The last words of wisdom dad ever said to me ring around my head as I steam from my flat.

'Son, a man's no a man until he's made this world a wee bit better before he leaves it.'

THE PEARHOOSE

This isn't the first nut-house I've been in. Although the devil docs and nazi nurses don't like us calling it that. 'It's a mental health hospital,' they say.

I say, if you name your dog Keith, it doesn't make it human.

My first experience inside one of these places occurred many years ago, when I was a lad of thirteen. That difficult age when you've few hairs on your balls and even less sense in your head. The age where you think you know better – that you've seen and done it all. How wrong I was.

That's why they've got me here today in this sun-drenched room with its perfect temperature, cool hues of grey and blue, comfortable seats, and tall plant in the corner. Very wholesome. I can almost feel the nourishment seeping through my bones, all the way to my soul.

Over the years they've called this room by many names – interview room, assessment room, consultation room. These days it's a 'safe space for healthy and open dialogue where patients can grow into their full potential'. They've called it the womb. I know better. It's an interrogation room. And if you ask me, I say this nut-house needs a hysterectomy.

The head nurse – affectionately known as Kim Jong-jill – finishes with the opening pleasantries and giving her professional assessment of my progress over the last year. Now it's down to business.

'So,' she says as she closes her file on me and sets it on the floor, 'is there anything you would like to add to that, Andrew?' Her cold, hazel eyes peer over rimless glasses.

Her two amigos sitting either side – Idiot Amin and Moron Hindley – keep scribbling away at their own folders perched upon their laps. Even though there's no physical barrier of a table between us, the mental barrier remains for all to feel – captive and captors alike.

I take a deep breath, exhale through pursed lips, lean back in the cushioned chair, and allow my eyes to drift skyward. They'll get no arguments from me. I'd learnt that the hard way. Still, I've got to make this believable. Else it'll be another year detained at Her Majesty's pleasure.

I shake my head and look her in the eye. 'No, Nurse Bradshaw, I think you've done an excellent job in summarising this past year.'

'Please, Andrew,' she says as she removes her glasses and slips them over the top button of her deep-blue tunic. 'I've told you before, I'm happy for you to call me Jillian.'

'And as I've told you before, I'd prefer to give you the respect you've earned by addressing you by the proper title.'

'As you wish,' she says with a smile that doesn't reach her eyes. 'If, then, I ask you to define your conduct over this last year in one word, what would that word be?'

'Changed,' I say, perhaps a little too quick.

Idiot Amin, the nut-house's head psychiatrist, lifts his eyes from his notes and stares at me before sharing a glance with Kim Jong-jill.

'I'd agree with that,' she says.

And it *is* true. I've been a good boy, have taken all my meds without a fight, have willingly participated in the various programmes, and have even volunteered to mentor some of the other patients. Previously, I fought tooth and nail not to participate in the pathology of this place. To my mind, I still don't. But if I can somehow convince these gatekeepers that I've improved and am now a willing passenger on their road to recovery, then maybe the outcome will be different this time.

'Although,' she continues, '*changed* is a very open word. People can, and do, change for the worse.'

'Can I speak frankly?' I say, noticing Idiot Amin's attention is still on me.

'Please do,' Kim Jong-jill says.

'I'm under no illusion that the vast majority of my time here has been...'

'Less than productive?' she offers.

'...I was going to say *atrocious* or *despicable* or *contemptible*.' I sigh and give them a remorse filled expression that would have the Academy chucking an Oscar my way. 'If I'm being honest, when I look upon the thirteen years I've spent here, I feel nothing but shame and embarrassment.'

'What shames you the most?'

'Everything. My whole attitude towards this place, and to you and your good staff, was nothing short of malevolent.'

'Now there's a strong word. Care to dig deeper as to why you behaved so?'

I nod and nibble my lower lip. 'I will, but please understand, it's difficult for me to relive those memories. I feel I've progressed greatly, and am in such a good place at the moment, but I'm always fearful of slipping back into that dark place.'

Idiot Amin pipes up, 'Voluntary exposure is by far the best treatment for overcoming fears.'

I nod in agreement. 'And, as Jung says, in order to become a well-rounded individual, one must be willing to face the shadow within and integrate it into their psyche.'

Idiot Amin's greying goatee flashes yellow stained teeth as his face breaks into a smile. 'Exactly.'

Moron Hindley pauses from her incessant scribbling. Her head cocks slightly in my direction. The moment I turn my attention to her she looks back at her notes and continues writing.

Where Idiot Amin is what you'd get if you asked someone to draw a shrink with his tweed jacket, checkered shirt, corduroy trousers, thick glasses, and wavy hair, Moron Hindley is rather different. I'd say she's around thirty-five, and everything about her screams high-flying business type. From her blonde hair tied up in a bun, to her white blouse with just the right amount of top buttons open, all the way to her grey pencil-skirt that reaches the appropriate side of her knees. Even from here, her flowery perfume entices my nostrils like something from a Disney film. The only jewellery she wears are pearl earrings and a slim silver watch. There's no ring on her finger either – motherhood is so 1950's. Moron Hindley isn't part of the state-run health service. She's a private consultant sometimes hired by the authorities to deal with unusual cases. Apparently, she's taken a keen interest in me.

Can't say I blame her. If it were me sat where she is, I'd be intrigued with a fantastical story such as mine. And just like every shrink, police officer, juror, friend, and family member I've tried to convince of my innocence over the years, I'd be calling bullshit too.

'So,' I say, 'where to begin?' I straighten myself in my seat and clasp my hands together. 'As you are all well-aware, when first admitted, I was of the mindset that I shouldn't be here. Clichéd, but I was certain I was the only sane person in the loony bin.'

Kim Jong-jill raises her eyebrows. 'Andrew—'

'I know, I know, it's a mental health hospital, but that's how I felt back then.'

'And now?'

I sigh. 'Now I see the error of my ways as clear as day.'

'Why the change of opinion?'

'I think seeing so many people coming here over the years, the vast majority of them all thinking the same as me, made me realise we can't *all* have been wrongly committed.'

'So, you no longer believe you shouldn't be here?'

'No,' I lie with a shake of the head.

'So then, Andrew, what's your take now on the...*incident* that led to your mental breakdown?'

I moisten my lips and gulp. Moron Hindley closes her folder and sets it down. I glance in her direction as she adjusts herself in her seat. Her dark, emotionless eyes lock onto mine. This is what she's here for – her money shot, so to speak. A bead of sweat streams down the inside of my arm. I just *know* she's waiting for me to slip up – to give any sign that I still hold true as to what happened that day.

An eerily familiar sight of a flock of birds fleeing the nearby woods catches my eye and chills my blood. I turn and gaze out the window as my heart quickens at the wave of memories flooding over me.

* * *

We were in the last weekend of an unusually hot Easter break from school, and were struggling to fill the lengthening days. We spent most of our time swimming in the river or hanging about the rope swing in a nearby wood. We called it the jungle swing, and if you'd seen the mass of weans climbing the huge oak tree it hung from, you'd have thought you were watching a troop of monkeys. Once in a while the council would come and take it down, but someone, and no one knew who, would put a new one back up. My pal Shug said it was a local paedophile who did it so he could watch us from the bushes. But Shug usually talked more shite than a drunk politician having a stroke, so no one paid any attention.

So on a Saturday evening, while all the other kids were still getting fed, me and my pal Matty made our way there. Matty had been at mine for dinner that day, as he had most days during the break. With no free school meal and smack a bigger priority than food for his mum, it was the only sustenance he got.

We were first to arrive, or so we thought. But when a penny bounced off Matty's head and hit my shoulder, we knew Shug had beaten us there. We looked up in unison to see him perched high above us upon the big branch that held the swing.

'About time, dickheads,' he said with a cheesy grin.

We returned the pleasantries and told him to come down. He did, but not before pulling the swing up before we could grab it. We told him he was out of order for wrapping it up out of reach.

He just laughed and said, 'Dry your eyes.'

Shug was the best climber. Most of the other kids wouldn't be able to climb up and unfurl the rope, and he knew it. He was also the best fighter so our objections weren't too forceful. We left before the angry masses arrived to find the swing out of reach. Shug led the way through the narrow path, trodden from thousands of wean's feet. He informed us that the evening's plans had changed.

'We're not staying at mine anymore,' he said.

'We're not?' I said, stopping in my tracks as Matty bumped up behind me.

Shug continued walking and swinging a stick at the overgrown bushes. 'Nope.'

'Wait a minute,' I said.

Shug stopped and turned.

'I've already told my mum I'm staying at yours. You know what she's like. If I go home now, she'll think something's wrong.'

'Calm down,' he said, adjusting his cap. 'You're not going home.'

The smirk on his face told me he was up to something, and when Shug got up to things, we all usually ended up in trouble.

I knew I'd regret asking but curiosity beat me. 'Where we going then?'

'You, me, and that meth-baby behind you are doing the streets tonight.'

'Hoi!' Matty protested.

I sighed and shook my head. 'What, walking the streets aimlessly all night? Sounds about as exciting as watching paint dry at your gran's birthday party.'

'No it doesn't, it sounds brilliant. No parents telling us what to do, when to be home, when to go to bed. Sounds like freedom to me.'

'No bother, Braveheart,' Matty said.

I laughed.

Shug scowled. 'No bother...junkie-heart.'

'That's a shit comeback,' Matty correctly said. 'Doesn't even make sense.'

'Yes it does, it means that—'

'Never mind that,' I said, interrupting the bickering pair before it escalated. 'The fact of the matter is, I'm not doing the streets. End of.'

'Well, you kind of have to,' Shug said smugly. 'Think about it. You've told your mum you're staying at mine. If you go back now with no reason, it'll be months before she lets you out of sight again.' He had a point but I still wasn't convinced. Then he hit us with the mother of all persuasions. 'And anyway, if you don't, I'll tell everyone how you were too scared to do it. Do you really want to be known as a chicken, a feartie, a shitebag even?'

'Nah,' I said, shaking my head. 'You wouldn't do that because that would make you a grass.'

He never flinched. 'Try me.'

School was tough enough without being branded a coward. I stared him out for a moment, trying to gauge if he was bluffing. He looked serious.

'But...' I said, trying to come up with a plausible excuse.

Shug's face scrunched up as he crossed his arms and tilted his head. 'But what?'

'We're all dressed in shorts and T-shirts. It'll be baltic when the sun goes down.'

'Look, I wasn't going to say till later, but I've got somewhere...*special* lined up for us to go.'

'Where?'

'Don't spaz out, but I know a way into the poorhouse.'

Before I could tell him how stupid an idea that was, Matty said, 'What's a poorhouse?'

'You should know,' Shug said. 'You live in one.'

'Good one,' Matty said, pushing his milk-bottle specs up the bridge of his nose. 'Andy, what's a poorhouse?'

'It's not a poorhouse,' I said. 'It's a nut-house. Or at least it was.'

'Potato, potahto,' Shug said. 'Are yous up for it?'

'I still don't know what it is!' Matty said, throwing his skinny arms up.

I told him, 'It's the old Crawswood Asylum up by Marshside.'

'Where they found the bodies?' Matty said, the excitement clear in his voice.

'Exactly!' Shug said. 'What do you say?'

Matty was into horror films and anything dark so it was no surprise he said, 'I'm up for that!'

'Well?' Shug said, looking at me.

I glanced at Matty. He looked like a puppy who wanted to go walkies. I shook my head and said, 'Fine,' before barging past Shug. 'But if we're doing it, we're doing it now, before it gets dark.'

I marched on in front ignoring Shug's comment about me being afraid of the dark.

We made our way along the river trail, over the blue bridge, up the moor, through the abandoned racecourse, and onto the golf course, until all we could see of our town was the tops of the high flats and churches.

Shug had wanted to skirt around the golf course and through the nature reserve, saying it was quicker. It wasn't. He'd been trying to slow us down all the way. Like stopping for fags when we could have walked and smoked at the same time or taking ages in the sweet shop. He was also constantly checking his phone and even walked away from us to speak with someone unheard. Bear in mind, this was a time when phones weren't smarter than people, and no one spent every waking second staring at them.

We chatted about what we knew, or at least what we'd heard, about the poorhouse. It had been all over the local news, even making a brief appearance in the national papers, when workers surveying it in preparation for houses being built there found an unmarked mass grave. The poorhouse was a remnant from Victorian times and began life as a workhouse for the poor. Think *Oliver Twist* without the singing. It soon expanded and morphed into an asylum. Back then, that meant a place the dregs were sent to be forgotten by polite society – invalids, elderly, criminally insane, even young women who'd fallen pregnant out of wedlock. It was common practice in these institutes that if one of the inmates died and no one claimed their body, they would be buried on the hospital grounds in a pauper's grave.

When he wasn't on his phone or dragging his heels, Shug embellished the story. He said they used to carry out all types of horrific experiments on the inmates, and when they went wrong and people died, they put them into a secret grave, and this was the one the workers found.

When we asked him how he knew all this, he *reliably* told us that his sister's, boyfriend's, pal's, gran used to work there before it was abandoned. According to Shug, she swears that the place is haunted by the tortured souls who'd perished there over the years. Apparently, she'd also witnessed many strange and spooky happenings – things falling from the walls, doors slamming violently shut, footsteps in empty corridors, banging from empty rooms, and even screams. He'd also heard that a nurse who had to do a night shift on her own ended up deranged and became an inmate herself.

Matty lapped all this up, even throwing in his own tuppence worth. He said it's likely that if people were tortured to death in that place, their spirit would remain seeking vengeance.

All chattering story-telling ceased when we reached the metal heras-fencing the workers had erected. We scrambled over this first line of defence with little effort. The next two would require a more deft approach. Between the fencing and tall brick wall topped with broken glass and vandal paint, lay a moat of thorn bushes.

Shug led us around the perimeter fencing until a gap appeared in the bushes. We turned into it and faced a rusting, iron gate. It was padlocked with a heavy chain, and would've been an easy climb for us if not for the barbed wire running along its pointy summit. We followed Shug as he pushed through the tiny gap between the thorn bushes and wall. We fought our way back in the direction we'd come, and I started to regret wearing shorts.

By the time Shug stopped and said, 'Here we are,' my legs were in tatters.

An old blanket had been thrown over the wall, offering some protection from the deterrents above.

Shug whispered, 'Give me and Matty a punt up and we'll pull you up.'

I squatted with my back against the wall and clasped my hands together at waist height. Shug stepped onto my hands and I pushed him up onto the wall. After helping Matty up, they both leaned over and held out a hand. I took them and scrambled up the wall. Shug and Matty lowered themselves from the wall as I paused. A flock of birds rose from the woods and flew towards the blood-red sun, already setting behind the pointy peaks of the Isle of Nara. I shivered and lowered myself into the poorhouse's grounds.

It seemed darker and colder this side of the wall, with every footstep echoing louder. It reminded me of an end-of-the-world film. Over-grown bushes and trees littered the grounds. Moss and grass carpeted the once concrete ground. Piles of stone, wood, and other rubble dotted the area. There was a mishmash of various small buildings, most of their roofs having long given up the ghost.

We ignored these shells and made for the main hospital building. The grey-stone, U-shaped, two storey building seemed more structurally sound. It still had most of its pitched slate roof, and even one or two of the upper-floor windows were still intact. The rest had fallen victim to vandals, and the lower windows were boarded up with metal sheeting – council curtains, we called them. An empty bell tower perched above the main entrance, which had also been secured with a metal door.

Shug led us around the back of the building to a staircase that descended below ground. The crunch of broken glass echoed around the stairwell as we crept down the concrete stairs. At the foot of the stairs was another metal door, though this one was wedged open slightly. It had also been spray painted in red, block capitals – 'LEEVE THIS PLACE NOW. BEFORE ITS TO LATE'.

'Right,' Shug whispered. 'You two squeeze in first, then push the door open from the inside as much as you can for me.'

Matty didn't need telling twice as he scurried into the darkness. I hesitated.

'If you're scared to go in, then you can wait outside,' Shug said with a smirk.

'I'm not scared, it's just...what if something happens to us inside? No one knows where we are, and thanks to you, my mum thinks I'm—'

'Ha! So, you're scared of your mum? That's even worse. Why don't you get your mummy to come and hold your hand?'

'I'd prefer if your mum came and held my dick.'

Shug's brow furrowed and eyes narrowed. 'Don't talk about my mum.'

'Well, don't call me a shitebag then. Plus, it's pitch-black in there. How are we supposed to see?'

Shug smiled as he produced a small torch from his pocket. 'Should've been in the scouts, me.'

I shook my head and sighed as I held out a hand.

Shug pulled his in. 'Nope. My torch so I get to hold it.'

I squeezed through the door wondering why I hung around with a prick like Shug.

The thick air inside felt like when you walk into the swimming baths, and it smelt like the concrete pipe that spews brown mulch into the river. I couldn't see Matty and nearly shat myself when he stepped out of the darkness and touched my arm, whispering, 'Boo.'

Shug tried squeezing in while telling us to help. He was bigger than us but not in an overweight way, more like he'd been held back a year or two at school. Me and Matty put our backs into the door and opened it enough for Shug to get in.

'Urgh,' he said as he stumbled into the darkness. 'What's that smell?'

'Andy's arse,' Matty said.

'Your breath,' I shot back.

'Your mum's breath,' he returned.

'Your mum's breath after rimming my arse,' I said, ending the battle.

Shug clicked his torch on and shone it on my face. I squinted, held up my hand, and told him to pack it in.

He just laughed and said, 'Follow me.'

Shug went first while me and Matty followed closely behind. We walked a short corridor before climbing a set of concrete stairs. I only caught glimpses from the torch light but could feel the rubbish strewn around underfoot. We passed through a doorless doorway at the top of the stairs and into a large, open area. Fading daylight seeped through the many holes in the roof, but it wasn't enough to see the entirety of the area we stood in.

We huddled together as Shug shone his torch around.

We were in the centre of what looked like a foyer. Countless doors surrounded us on the ground level. A balcony, broken only by a wide staircase at the far end, encircled us above. The place was a mess. Brown-stained ceilings sagged like giant blisters while wires hung from the parts damaged by fire. Yellowed walls peeled like the skin on my back after I fell asleep on the beach the previous summer. Broken chairs, old metal bed frames bent out of shape, and paper littered the floor.

'Looks like Matty's house,' Shug commented.

Matty cursed him, but he had a point, though I'd never say that to Matty.

'Okay,' I said, trying to conceal any apprehension. 'That's us done it. We're in and there's nothing much to see. In fact, it's a complete and utter shit-hole. Probably littered with dirty needles. Let's go.'

Shug sighed before turning his torch on me. 'You're worse than my wee sister. Here.' He directed the beam towards the ground and held out the torch. 'Will this make you stop acting like a baby?'

Even though I wanted to, I knew taking it would be seen as an admission of my fear and I'd never hear the end of it. 'Keep it.'

'You're such a brave boy,' Shug said. 'Come on, let's explore.' He turned and made his way across the foyer.

As we followed, Matty nudged my arm and flicked his lighter on. The orange glow sent shadows dancing across his face. He nodded at the lighter, asking the silent question if I wanted it. I shook my head and his ghostly face disappeared into the darkness.

Shug led us past doorway after doorway until we were at the far corner just next to the stairs. We went through a door at the foot of the stairs and turned left. A smell like wet dog hung in the air, and it was slippery underfoot. It wasn't long before I'd lost all sense of where we were in that building. Or more importantly, where we were in relation to the exit. I was sure that corridor went underneath the stairs. The pungent, damp scent became more suffocating the further we went until I had to breathe out my mouth.

Now, it never clicked at the time, but Shug was acting strange. He seemed confident and unnerved. Far too sure of himself and where we were going in this maze of darkness. I think because my own mind was playing tricks on me I wasn't able to detect any tom-foolery afoot. It felt like being constantly watched by someone...or some*thing*. Always at my back, but never there when I looked. Every gruesome scene from every horror film I'd seen ran through my mind's eye. I was convinced I saw things move in the shadows, and only the greater fear of being teased again kept me from saying out loud.

We came to a door at the end of the corridor and Shug said, 'Let's see what's in here,' as if it were a random door he'd led us to.

My suspicions were roused that it wasn't random because he never even tried to open it. Instead, he crawled through the bottom half which had been kicked in. When I crouched low to scurry in, it became clear the smell of dampness and decay came from this room.

Shug slowly swept his torch around. The once-white walls had been enveloped by a colony of black mould spreading from between each tile. A large, partially smashed ceramic sink took up most of the far wall. Copper pipes jutted from the wall where once there were taps. In the middle, protruding from the ceiling like a giant robotic arm, was some kind of operating room light. Shug lowered the beam, revealing what the operating light used to shine upon. Matty sucked his breath in hard at the macabre sight. It looked more like a prop from a horror film than an operating table.

'See,' Shug said, 'I told you they used to experiment on them.'

Matty stepped forward to get a closer look. 'Look at these! Straps to hold the victims down. This is amazing. I want this in my room.'

'Check if there's any blood-stains,' Shug said as he joined him.

As I stood rooted to the spot, watching my two best pals drool over this thing like it was a new bike, I couldn't help wondering about all the people who *had* been bound to it over the years. Now, I was certain Shug's stories were bullshit, and I now knew he'd led us there to try and frighten us. Still, I couldn't help think, what if they *were* doing experiments on the inmates? All it takes is for one psycho doctor to get a job there – and they say evil-doers seek out positions of authority over vulnerable people – and he could live out his darkest, disturbed fantasies.

I wondered what it would be like knowing a monster has power over you and there is nothing you can do about it. After all, who's going to believe an inmate of a nut-house over a doctor?

A loud thud from above interrupted my troubling thoughts.

Matty and Shug stopped their excited chatter. I held my breath.

'Did you hear that?' Shug said.

'Yeah,' I said, 'probably a bird or somethi—'

More thuds came, like someone banging on the floor in the room directly above us.

'I don't think that's a bird,' Shug said.

'Could be a ghost,' Matty said, the hope clear in his voice.

Shug held his torch below his face as he backed towards the door. 'Ooohh...only one way to find out.'

He ducked under the door with Matty hot on his heels, leaving me alone in the dark, dank room of nightmares.

That unnerving sense of being watched returned and shocked me into action. As I made for the door, I'm certain I heard a hushed, menacing voice growl, '*My* hospital.'

In my panic to escape, I smacked my head against the upper half of the door. Dazed and scared, I scampered towards the light at the end of the tunnel.

I caught up with the pair at the top of the stairs, breathless and amazed my ankles were still intact. I was about to give them an earful when Shug signalled for me to be quiet.

'I think it came from in here,' he said.

'You think?' I said. 'Don't give me it. Just get the door opened and let's see.'

He could barely keep a straight face as he opened the creaky door. This room wasn't as dark. Fading daylight seeped in from the edges of the council curtains.

I stepped inside and burst out laughing. A large circle of candles lay on the floor, surrounding a blood-red pentagram that had been crudely spray-painted onto the floor.

'Wow,' I said, slowly clapping. 'Is this the best you can do?'

Shug feigned confusion. 'What do you mean?'

I shook my head. 'We *just happened* to wander into the experimentation room you had been prattling on about. Then a bang *just happened* to come from the room above it. A room you *just happened* to find far too easily. Then it turns out this room *just happens* to be some kind of devil-worshiper's lair.' I tutted 'Fuck sake, even the paint's the same colour as the warning sign outside, and I know that was you as you can't spell to save your life.'

Shug stood with his mouth open but it was Matty who spoke first. He looked serious – scared, even. 'Guys, it doesn't matter if it was done as a joke or for real. It's a dangerous game when you play with the occult. We should get out. Now.'

Before I could call him out for being in on the prank, a high-pitched screech like a feral animal followed by a scream caused me to jump.

'Right, Shug,' I seethed. 'Who've you got in on it?'

He couldn't contain himself anymore and started laughing. 'It's Rab and Josey, from my football team.'

'Is that who you were calling on the way here?'

He nodded. 'I gotcha, didn't I?'

I could've punched the beaming smirk off his face. 'Best. Prank. *Ever.*'

'I can see one of them,' Matty said.

I turned.

Matty stood just outside the door, looking along the balcony. 'Josey! Rab! We know it's you. Come out, the games up.'

I joined him and peered over his shoulder. A motionless silhouette stood further along the balcony. The moment Shug joined us and directed his torchlight in its direction, it disappeared into a room.

Shug strode toward where it was, calling for them to come out. He slowed as he reached the room, as if in anticipation of them jumping out.

Me and Matty stopped a few paces back. If they planned on giving us a fright, it would be Shug bearing the brunt.

He jumped in front of the open door with his torch held out like a soldier clearing a hostile building. The glee on his face turned to hesitancy.

'Guys?' He jerked the torch around in ever more erratic movements before stopping. A look of horror crept across his face. 'What the...?'

Here we go again. 'You're persistent, I'll give you that.'

'No, straight up. Come and look.'

He genuinely looked shaken, but I wasn't born yesterday so I let Matty take the lead while I braced myself. Mercifully, the jump scare never came. In hindsight, I'd have taken that over what I saw in there a million times over.

In the middle of the room, illuminated by Shug's torch, was the creepiest thing I'd yet seen – an ancient, rusting wheelchair with a doll sat upon it. Its body burnt to a crisp, while its head, seemingly untouched from the flames that had engulfed its body, held in its outstretched arms.

A nervous laugh escaped my lips. 'That's creepier than your Uncle Eddie. You should have taken us here first. That would defin—'

'This wasn't us,' Shug hissed.

'We need to get out of here,' Matty said, the earlier excitement in his voice replaced by anxiety.

'Where's your pals?' I asked.

'That's the thing.' He swept his torch around, revealing an empty room with no other doors. 'They're not fucking here.'

'Call them.'

'I don't have any talk time left.'

I pulled my phone out. 'Give me their number, and be quick, my battery's about to die.'

Before he got the chance to give me their number, a creaking from within the room caused us all to inhale sharply and hold our breath.

Shug slowly directed the light back into the room. The shaky beam fell upon the wheelchair. It had moved from the centre of the room, sitting right at the door, and the doll's head was gone.

We froze before a thud to our left made us all jump.

Shug turned his torch in the direction of the sound.

There, within touching distance, lay the mutilated corpse of one of Shug's pals.

The flight defence mechanism kicked in and we fled for the stairs.

The next few minutes are a blur in my mind, like a dream, or more likely, a surreal nightmare. I operated on raw instinct.

I led the way. Thundering footsteps echoed. Screams and shouts hurt my ears. Shadows menaced all around. It felt like my heart would burst from my chest, and it was as though it was the first time I'd used my legs. I was sure every door I passed would be my last, and I prayed I wouldn't trip or stumble. Shamefully, a wee bit of me hoped one of my pals would.

I reached the stairs and descended them at least four at a time. I reached the bottom as a blood-curdling scream I can still hear to this day made me glance up. There, suspended high above me in mid-air like a bird of prey, was Matty.

The moment my eyes drank in this unbelievable sight, he came crashing down to the ground with accelerated force. The sound of his body splatting on the concrete before me will live with me forever.

I screamed and dropped to my knees.

Shug flew past us, striding over Matty's prone, misshapen body.

Now, I was certain Matty was dead, but I couldn't bring myself to leave him there. I shouted for Shug to stop, to come back and help, but – and I don't blame him – he never did.

My trembling hands reached out for Matty before a sound from behind caused me to freeze again. It was like being under water and was coming down the stairs fast, getting louder by the second. I closed my eyes as it reached me. A current of stale air whooshed past like when a train approaches an underground platform.

Like a scared-shitless Arnold Schwarzenegger, I whispered, 'I'll be back,' scrambled to my feet, and sprinted towards Shug's flashlight.

He was almost at the entrance to the stairwell we'd entered by.

He never made it.

When he was only a few strides from the door, the body of Shug's other pal dropped from the balcony. The rope wrapped around his neck jolted his limp body, causing him to swing back and forth in front of the exit.

Shug screamed and took off in another direction.

I did the same, charging into the first room I came to. I fumbled around in the dark, pleading, begging for a way out.

I eventually came across a metal locker. My trembling hands found the handle. I opened it and jumped inside, closing the door quietly behind me.

I fished my phone from my pocket and dialled my home number. It seemed a lifetime before the ringing tone sounded. It seemed an eternity before my mum answered.

'Andrew, what's wrong?' was all I got before the battery died.

That's when the tears started. I don't think they stopped all night. I slumped down inside of that locker and curled into the fetal position. My shorts and boxers were sodden – exactly when I pished myself, I'm unsure of.

I lay there all night, shaking and whimpering like a whipped pup, tormented by the terrible sounds from outside. Banging and screaming, moaning and wailing, and worst of all, the laughter. Hysterical it was, manic even. Sickly scents, like the sewerage plant on the outskirts of town but worse, wafted into my prison. At one point I was certain I could smell burning.

Early on in my ordeal, I thought I heard a window smash. I prayed it was Shug and he'd gotten out. That he would be racing from this place to get help. I fantasized he'd return with our parents, the police, the army, *anyone* able to get me out of there alive. I think that's what kept me going because at one point a strange part of me wanted to step out and face whatever prowled this awful building. This wasn't some misguided bravery on my part. It was more like I just wanted it to be over.

No rescuers came.

The realisation that I would have to get myself out of there scared me more than anything. I finally summoned the courage when silence reigned, although not straight away. I must have stayed there for at least an hour after the din ceased.

The first step from that locker was the hardest thing I've ever had to do.

I tiptoed to the door and peered outside. The coast seemed clear.

Sticking to the wall, I crept towards the exit like a mouse, keeping my eyes down.

I squeezed past the hanging corpse and descended the stairs.

Every step I took seemed annoyingly loud, and I was certain I'd be grabbed from the darkness at any moment.

Mercifully, I wasn't.

I barged out the door into beautiful daylight, scrambled up the stairs, and sprinted around that building faster than I've ever ran before.

Halfway across the courtyard a bell tolled behind me. I turned. The bell tower was still empty.

That's when I saw Shug. His lifeless body lay slumped out an upper-floor window, impaled by a large, pointy piece of glass.

Retching and gasping for air with tears stinging my eyes, I turned and ran. Sick and bile filled my mouth before I reached the gate. I never stopped to be sick. I kept running with my cheeks puffed out like a hamster and flung myself over it, slicing my legs and hands on the barbed wire. I landed on the opposite side, dropped to my knees, and heaved my guts all over the grassy concrete with a splat.

#

I notice I've been tracing the web of scars across my palms before realising Kim Jong-jill is saying my name.

'Yes?' I say.

'I asked, what's your take now on the incident that led to your mental breakdown?'

I look her in the eye, hoping she doesn't detect I'm about to lie. 'I made it all up.'

Her eyes light up and nostrils flare. 'And the four boys? It *wasn't* the ghosts who killed them?'

'No.'

'So, Andrew, who was it that butchered them?'

That, I do not know the answer to. I do know what she wants to hear. The only answer that'll satisfy them all. The only answer that'll move me in the direction of getting out of here.

'I did.'

WARM CALLERS

DING-DONG!

I turn my music down and mindlessly head for the door before the realisation hits. Anyone I care for doesn't abide by such formalities as doorbells.

Too late.

I'm in my hallway. Only my front door stands between me and the two young men outside. Unfortunately, it's a half-panel glass door.

Maybe if I moonwalk back out of sigh—

Fuck. They've seen me. Too late to hide now. Or is it? It's quite sunny out today. Perhaps the glare from the sun is preventing them from seeing int—

Bastard.

One of them smiles and waves. Their charcoal suits, crisp white-shirts, and fifties side-parting tells me exactly what they're after.

I wonder what they'd do if I remained as still as a Buckingham Palace guard? How long before they'd take the hint? I sigh inside. This lot are more dogged than I could ever be. There's no doubt I'd be the first to blink. I curse under my breath and grudgingly open the door.

'Good morning, sir,' the taller one says with all the exuberance only found in puppies and simpletons. 'How are you today?' He flashes a toothy grin.

'I'm okay.'

'Just okay? I find it difficult to believe anyone can be anything less than joyous when the good lord blesses us with such a fine day.'

Here we go. 'Look, I don't mean to be rude, but I'm *so* busy just now. I really don't have the tim—'

'Too busy for God?'

There it is. 'Why? Is she here?' I pop my head out the door and glance up and down my street. 'I don't see her?'

The smaller one fake laughs. '*He* is all around us, friend. He is in the plants, the trees, the birds and the bees. He is in here'—he points at his temple before cupping his heart—'and in here. But only if you open up and let him in. Tell me, friend, *have* you experienced the unconditional love and sheer bliss one can only attain through the words of our lord and saviour, Jesus Christ?'

My mind casts back to an experience so mystically beautiful and awe-inspiring, words fail to describe it. I look the puppet in the eye and speak to him in a way he's likely seldom experienced – truthfully.

'Pal,' I say, 'who needs God when there's Pink Floyd and Magic Mushrooms in this world?'

The pair look like marionettes that have just had their strings cut as I close the door.

I go into my living room and search through my music library, seeking my church, my religion, my God.

77

TWO PEAS IN A POD

Once upon a time, in a special, magical place, far far away, Little Joseph delivered a rousing speech to all fifty million of his brothers.

'Comrades,' he called, capturing the attention of the testy sperm jostling for position in the epididymis of the left testicle. 'Comrades, it appears our time of oppression nears end. Can you not feel the uprising?'

The fifty million sperm cheered and whistled and danced with delight in the testicular fluid.

'Da, comrades,' Little Joseph continued. 'Revolution. Is. Cumming!'

His fifty million brothers cheered so loud, Little Joseph feared they might blow their load too soon. He raised his flagellum to calm the excitable sperm, gleefully bouncing on their own tails.

'Comrades, I share your enthusiasm, I truly do. But know this – only by working together do we have any chance of vanquishing bourgeoisie and realising our utopia. I will not lie to you, comrades. This journey will be difficult one, with danger at every turn. There will be many obstacles placed before us, but I believe we shall overcome if we strive as collective. One measly sperm on its own can do nothing. But fifty million working together for common good? That, comrades, is what shall make us unstoppable. We shall unite into fifty-million-strong hand, and fist our way to promised land!'

Meanwhile, in the epididymis of the right testicle, Little Adolph was busy giving his own rousing speech.

'Volker,' he called to the fifty million sperm lined up in neat rows before him. 'Your struggle is my struggle, and my struggle is our struggle. It appears our time of oppression nears ze end. Can you not feel ze time is upon us to bust forth from zese confines and take ze rightful living space ve need?'

His fifty million brothers stamped their tails in unison.

'Ze war to cum cannot be won alone. Nein. Our strength lies in our speed and in our brutality. Fifty million pure sperm moving as one, striking with ze speed and ferocity of ze lightning bolt? Zat, my dear ubersperm, is an unstoppable force zat shall propel us all to ze promised realm, thus giving us ze living space ve are due.'

The fifty million master-sperm hailed their supreme leader by raising and holding their tails aloft.

Just then, Little Adolph and his fifty million brothers were withdrawn from their crushing confines in the epididymis of the right testicle. They were propelled in great waves along the right vas deferens – swimming headlong and focused on the task ahead. They reached the right ejaculatory duct, got drenched in sticky warm seminal fluid, before spurting from the ejaculatory duct and into the urethra.

Little Adolph's lightning war faltered when he saw Little Joseph and his comrades bust from the left ejaculatory duct in great numbers.

Little Adolph and Little Joseph locked eyes, and it was like peering into a mirror for both of them. Like sharks with the scent of blood in the water, they darted forwards – eyes narrowed in furious concentration. They stopped before colliding and circled each other, their tails flicking with menace. Their respective fifty million brothers lined up across from each other like opposing factions in a medieval battle.

'Vas ist das!' roared Little Adolph.

'What is "vas ist das"?' Little Joseph said.

'Das!' Little Adolph pointed his tail at Little Joseph's fifty million brothers. 'Vas ist das!'

'Comrade, "das" is great downtrodden proletariat-sperm. United as one to smash stinking oppressor.'

'Nein, nein, nein, nein, nein! *Ve* are ze great downtrodden master-sperm. United as one to smash ze filthy oppressor. I sugges—nein, I *command* you take your rabble back under ze stone from which you came.'

'We, the great worker-sperm, take orders from no one.' Little Joseph turned to his brothers. 'Comrades, if these ruffians so much as *attempt* to block relentless march to great utopia, I command you all to smash them equally.'

Little Joseph and Little Adolph continued bickering as they were shot into the warm, wet vagina, along with their respective fifty-million-strong flock. Too occupied with seeing an enemy in the other, Little Joseph and Little Adolph were unaware of how fast they were slipping through the cervical mucus towards real danger.

Little Joseph sighed and rolled his eyes as Little Adolph went off on another rant about his sperm being superior, finally noticing the approaching danger.

'Comrade,' Little Joseph said to Little Adolph. 'It appears we have common enemy.' Little Joseph pointed his tail towards the fast-approaching cervix – the oppressive white blood-cells lurking beyond with menace.

'Scheisse,' Little Adolph said. 'Comrade – as you are so fond of saying – I suggest a non-aggression pact until ve rid ourselves of ze common enemy.'

'Da, comrade, I agree.'

Both Little Joseph and Little Adolph marvelled at their guile in outsmarting the other as they agreed to their alliance with their tails crossed behind their backs.

As they passed through the choke point of the cervix and into the killing fields of the uterus, Little Joseph and Little Adolph commanded their fifty million brothers to form a defensive perimeter around them. Each ordered their respective gaggle of ideologues to fight for the common good and, if required, sacrifice themselves to protect their glorious leaders. Each of Little Joseph and Little Adolph's fifty million brothers did as commanded without question.

The campaign through the uterus towards the promised land of the fallopian tubes was a brutal, bloody struggle. Little Joseph and Little Adolph cowered behind their brainless but brave cannon-fodder as they flung themselves against the evil white blood-cells. Like lambs to the slaughter, they perished in their millions.

One hundred million useful idiots soon became ninety million, sixty million, ten million, until only a thin white line stood between Little Joseph and Little Adolph and the evil white blood-cells.

At this point, Little Adolph noticed the attack from the evil white blood-cells was faltering. The promised realm of the right fallopian tube was in reach, and so like a good little sociopath, he seized the initiative.

'Great ubersperm of ze right testicle!' called Little Adolph. 'Ve have broken ze back of ze evil white blood-cells attack. I command you all to wage ze lightning war against ze impure sperm of ze left testicle. Leave none alive zat call themselves comrade!'

As one, the great master-sperm of the right testicle turned against the great proletariat-sperm of the left testicle, encircling them and routing them without mercy.

Little Adolph rejoiced in the shock on Little Joseph's face as he became entrapped in the centre of his proletariat-sperm, bravely resisting the onslaught from Little Adolph's master-sperm.

'Fight, comrades!' Little Joseph called. 'Protect your leader. Give no quarters and smash these double-crossing vermin!'

Little Adolph smiled wryly at Little Joseph. He held his tail aloft in salute at a worthy adversary who, under different circumstances, might have been a brother, before swimming away out of sight up the right fallopian tube.

As the cilia pushed Little Adolph further and further along the right fallopian tube, he became more and more convinced he had chosen the correct path. The increasing temperature and sweet, alluring scent of the chemoattractants beckoned him towards the promised realm. Little Adolph smiled and swam a little faster towards his goal.

Meanwhile, back in the forsaken killing fields of the uterus, the destruction was almost absolute. Barely a sperm – master or proletariat – remained alive.

Little Joseph surveyed the bleak desolation with sorrow. The few remaining proletariat-sperm bravely holding out against the few remaining master-sperm, while all around, a sea of death and destruction surrounded them. Little Joseph felt pangs of guilt, horror and shame... that he had allowed Little Adolph to make a fool out of him.

Despondent, Little Joseph abandoned his brothers and slunk away in the direction of the left fallopian tube, hoping against all hope that Little Adolph had chosen the wrong path.

As the cilia pushed Little Joseph further and further along the left fallopian tube, he became more and more convinced he *had* chosen the correct path. The increasing temperature and sweet, alluring scent of the chemoattractants beckoned him towards utopia. Little Joseph smiled at the thought of Little Adolph furiously ranting in the barren right fallopian tube, and swam a little faster towards his goal.

Meanwhile, over in the right fallopian tube, Little Adolph's outer layer went into capacitation, and his tail into hyperactivation as the glorious ovum came into sight. He smiled with glee at his wit and cunning as he broke through the ovum's cumulus oophorus, penetrated its membrane, and fused his nucleus with that of the ovum.

Back in the left fallopian tube, Little Joseph's outer layer also went into capacitation, and his tail into hyperactivation as a second glorious ovum came into sight. He smiled with glee at his wit and cunning as he broke through the ovum's cumulus oophorus, penetrated its membrane, and fused his nucleus with that of the ovum.

* * *

Approximately nine months after the battle of Uterusgrad, Mrs Abrams screamed and writhed and dug her nails into Mr Abrams' hand. Although his philanthropistic endeavours had financed the state-of-the-art hospital they were in, she still sought to give him a tiny sample of the pain that currently wracked her body.

'You're doing great,' said the midwife between Mrs Abram's legs. 'One more big push and the baby will be here.'

'The *first* baby will be here,' spat Mrs Abrams. 'Then I'll have to do it all over again.'

'Come on now, honey,' Mr Abrams sheepishly said. 'You can do this, I know you ca—'

'Don't you "come on honey" me!' Mrs Abrams said. 'I swear, by Yahweh and all things holy, if you ever come near me again, I'll—aaarrrggghhh!'

'That's it!' called the midwife. 'Keep pushing. Almost there...'

The white-hot pain in Mrs Abrams' abdomen receded as her first child slid into this world.

'Come here, Mr Abrams,' said the midwife.

Mr Abrams prised his wife's fingers open and went to the foot of the bed. He froze, open-mouthed at his firstborn laying in the midwife's arms before him.

A nurse had clamped the umbilical cord and handed him the sterile scissors.

'Cut here,' she said, pointing between the clamps. She clicked her fingers. 'Mr Abrams, stay in the game. Cut here.'

Feeling light-headed, Mr Abrams did as commanded before scuttling back to the head of the bed.'

'Is it okay?' Mrs Abrams asked Mr Abrams. 'Is it a boy or a girl?'

Mr Abrams stammered with his mouth open.

'Is it okay?' demanded Mrs Abrams.

'Your baby's fine, Mrs Abrams,' said the midwife. 'Now, let's see about getting baby number two out.'

After another painful delivery, Mrs Abrams lay panting and sweating on the hospital bed, waiting to meet her twin babies.

After cleaning and checking over the babies, the midwife and nurse brought them wrapped in white shawls to meet their parents.

'Mr and Mrs Abrams,' said the midwife. 'It's my pleasure to introduce you to your twin boys.'

The midwife and nurse handed them a child each. Both Mr and Mrs Abrams were struck with awe and joy at meeting their children.

'Do you have names picked for them yet?' asked the nurse.

Mr and Mrs Abrams looked into each other's eyes and smiled.

'Yes, we do,' said Mrs Abrams. 'This one is Samuel.'

'And this one,' said Mr Abrams, 'is Solomon.'

Little Joseph and Little Adolph's bottom lips quivered before they both screamed at the top of their lungs.

BETWEEN BLACK AND WHITE

One yells X, the other cries Y
   But who holds the truth, and who tells the lie?
   Due process, critical thinking, were once what it took
   Now the mere accusation, and the world's core is shook

If truth is a sandwich, each opinion the bread
   The meat in the middle, is where all must be fed
   Truth is subjective, and highly abstract
   But in the wrong hands, can be used to attack

Moustache twirling villains, are easily caught
   Ones clothed in virtue, come harder to spot
   Witch hunts, inquisitions, consigned to the past
   Then a blink of an eye, and pitchforks are amassed

The links of our chain, are forged by the hand
   That covers our mouth 'til we parrot their brand
   For if we submit, to the rule of the mob
   Then all we hold dear, they surely will rob

A CHRISTMAS SURPRISE

Ah hate ma life. Aw the troops'll be getting on it at Jamsie's gaff, but wit am ah doin? Traipsing around the Christmas market wae ma gran. Brilliant. Ah bet Natalie's there. Bet that clown Tam will be tryin tae fire in aboot her. Fuck sake, man.

'Look at this, Charles,' ma gran says, holdin up some crap fae a stall. 'Our Rebecca would look so cute in this. What d'ye think?'

Ah couldnae give a fuck aboot an elf baby-grow. 'Definitely, Gran. That would be smashin.'

'I knew you'd like it, son,' she says, fishin her purse fae her handbag.

Ah sigh n glance tae the heavens. Flashin LEDs of a waving Santa catches ma eye. What a prick.

Don't get me wrong, ah love ma gran, and she's been takin me tae the Christmas market since ah wis a wee boy. But ah'm no a wee boy anymore. And why in the fuck did she have tae pick a Saturday night?

After gettin her change – a whole fuckin penny – fae the guy at the stall she turns. 'Right son, I think that's me sorted. I just need somethin for Angela's wee one. You know, the young lassie next door. She's always putting ma bins out, and helping with ma'—ah don't care, ah don't care—'but I'll just pick somethin up next time I'm in'—still don't care, ah want tae go home—'oh, and I need to get a bottle of gin for Mary. You know, ma bingo pal, she always gets me someth'— aww, here we go wae the bingo shite. Kill me now. My ears prick at the word 'home'.

'Wit?' ah say.

'I was saying, is there anything you want tae do before we go home?'

'No Gran, ah'm good, let's go.'

'Have ye done all yer Christmas shoppin?'

Fuck no. 'Almost, but ah don't need anythin fae here. Let's go.'

'Oh, I wonder what you've got yer old gran,' she says, rubbin her hands wae a mischievous look on her face. 'Somethin good?'

'You'll just have tae wait n see.' But if ye don't get yer arse in gear it'll be a one-way ticket tae Switzerland. 'C'moan, let's go.'

'What about the skating? You used to love scooting around the ice rink.'

Fuck me gently. She's like a Rottweiler wae a newborn in its jaws. Tam'll be balls deep by the time ah get tae that gaff. 'Nah, Gran, think ah'll give it a miss. Got a big game the morra. Don't want tae risk goin over on ma ankle.'

She shakes her head and tuts. 'You and your football. You need tae let yer hair down once in a while and enjoy yerself.'

If ah hadn't been dragged here, ma hair would be aw the way doon tae the fuckin grun by noo, n they'd be callin me Rapunzel. 'Wit can ah say, Gran. Ah'm keen as.'

'Ye are so,' she says wae a laugh. 'C'mere, son.' She hooks her arm ontae mine. 'Ma auld legs are no wit they used to be.'

A bit ay me dies inside as ah shuffle towards the train station wae a pensioner hangin ontae me. She looks like ET waddling along beside me wae her brown coat n headscarf. At least no cunt'll be here tae see me – they're aw at Jamsie's gaff. Still, best tae keep a low profile, just in case. I pull ma cap doon, collar up, and shove ma hands intae ma jacket pockets.

We eventually reach the stairs tae the station. Two big coppers wae guns stand at the foot ay the stairs, and two wae dugs are at the top. We climb the stairs slower than one ay they tools wae the green 'P' plates on their motor. Ah pull ma phone out – 18:25. See if we miss this train.

We get tae the top n ah nearly shite maself when wan ay the polis dugs starts barkin n strainin at its leash. Must no have liked the look ay me. Ah look at the copper holdin the snarlin dug back n ma heart sinks. He's lookin right at me, beckonin me wae wan finger.

Fan-fucking-tastic. Just wit ah need. Tam n Natalie'll be married wae children at this rate.

The dug shuts up when the copper commands it tae sit. He points towards a doorway away fae the stream ay people who're havin a right good gawk as they walk past. He passes the leash tae his colleague before joinin us.

'What's your name?' he says as he pulls a wee notepad fae his pocket.

'Chaz.'

'Do I look like one of yer pals?' he barks, scarier than the dug by his side.

'Naw,' ah say wae a shake ay the head. The day ah'm pals wae a copper is the day ah become a loner.

'Then give me the full name your parents gave you.'

'Show some respect, Charles,' ma gran says, cuffin me around the ear.

Ah stop maself askin the big copper tae do her wae assault. 'It's Charles McLeod.'

'Officer,' ma gran says in her best telephone voice. 'Is there something wrong?'

'Ma'am, we need to ask your...?'

'Grandson.'

'...grandson a few questions.' He turns his attention back tae me. 'How old are you, Charles?'

'Sixteen.'

'Do you have anything on you, you shouldn't have?'

Ah shake ma head. 'Naw.'

'Then you won't mind if we search you?'

Actually, ah do mind. 'Fill yer boots.'

'Empty your pockets, please.'

Ah rummage around in ma pockets, comin away wae a phone, some cash, keys, n a half-empty packet ay chewing gum.

'Do you have any sharps on yer person?' he says as he snaps on a pair ay they blue gloves doctors wear.

How deep is this copper plannin on searchin?

'Wit,' ah say, 'like needles?'

'Needles, knives, scissors, anything that could injure me.'

'Nah, this is aw ah've got.'

He either never heard me or didnae believe me as he has a right good rummage himself.

'Hold your arms out like this,' he says, mimicking the motion. 'And take off that cap.'

This is utter pish. Ah sigh n roll ma eyes, but do as commanded.

'The less attitude the easier this will be,' he says.

Easier for who, exactly?

His rubber protected fingers sweep through ma hair, behind ma ears, under ma collar, n along both arms. Ah gag at his cheap aftershave n rancid breath as his hawns reach around n down ma back. He sticks both thumbs in ma waistband n sweeps around until they meet at the front. He squats as he pats doon both legs – his fingers comin dangerously close tae ma pecker.

'Slip yer trainers off, pal.'

So we're pals now?

Cold concrete seeps through ma thin socks. He finishes inspectin ma gutties, n signals for me tae put them back on. He stands n looks at his colleague wae a puzzled look oan his face. The other copper shrugs then nods towards the dugs.

'There's one more thing before you can go, Charles.'

The train – along wae any chance ah had wae Natalie – is long gone so do wit ye want, ya cunt. 'Sure.'

'Is it okay if ma dog has a sniff around about you?'

'Officer,' ma gran says, her telephone voice gone, replaced by a slight hint ay annoyance. 'Is this necessary? We've got a train tae catch.'

'Ma'am, it won't take a minute. What do you say, Charl—'

'But we don't *have* a minute,' ma gran insists. 'I won't be missing my soaps so you can continue harassing my grandson. It's a bloody disgrace the way you lot treat teenagers. Always thinking they're uptae no good. Well let me tell you, sonny, it's not on, and your sergeant will be hearing about this, as well as my local councillors.'

Ha! Get them telt, Gran.

The big copper stands wae his arms crossed n head tilted, staring blankly at ma gran as she rants.

'Finished?' he says wae a raised brow.

Ma gran dusts doon her coat as if she'd just been in a fight. 'Quite.'

The copper turns his attention tae me. 'So, Charles, what do *you* say?'

Ahh fuck. Guess we're doin this pish then. Ah glance at the dug then back at the copper. 'Does it bite?'

A sleekit smile creeps over his face. 'Only if I tell her to.'

A copper wae a sense ay humour? They should put him on display. 'Fine.'

'Ka-ra,' he says, clickin his fingers in front ay me.

Kara springs into action and holds her snout high. She sniffs the air as she approaches...n keeps doing so as she passes me n comes tae a rest between me n ma gran. She puts her snout against gran's bag n freezes wae only her tail waggin.

What in the actual fuck?

The two coppers glance at each other, wide-eyed, afore turnin their attention on ma gran.

'Ma'am,' the first one says, 'is there something you'd like to tel—'

'Yes, yes, alright sonny,' she says as she unzips her bag. 'You know, I'm quickly becoming a cat person.'

If looks could kill, the dug wae its snout pressed against gran's handbag would be stone-dead.

'Kara, sit.'

Ma gran produces a wee jam-jar fae her bag – it's no filled wae jam.

'Wait till I see that boy,' she says. 'He telt me glass jars kept the smell contained.'

'Kara's sense of smell is much stronger than you'd think.'

'Is that right?' says ma gran. 'It's a pity she didnae have a cold.'

She hands him the jar – he looks like he's tryin tae keep fae laughin. The moment he unscrews the lid, we aw catch the scent Kara had picked up.

'Ma'am,' he says as his eyes dart tae me. 'Is this yours?'

'Less of the Ma'am, sonny, I'm no the queen. My name's Jean Nisbet, and yes, it's mine.'

Well fuck me sideways. Gran likes a smoke.

'Are you aware this is cannabis?'

'I hope it is, else that'll be another reason to chin that boy.'

The copper steals a glance at his colleague holdin the two dugs. He also looks to be fightin the urge tae laugh.

'And are you aware that cannabis is illegal?'

'Very...I'm also aware it shouldnae be. It's an absolute joke that they can say something so—'

'Look, Ma'am—'

'Jean.'

'—Jean, I'm no here to debate the law, I'm only here to enforce it. And right now, this is illegal. Right or wrong, one thing I do know, buying this lines the pockets of drug dealers.'

'Sonny, I've lined the pockets of the biggest drug dealers on the planet. For fifteen years I bought their junk – paracetamol, co-codamol, ibuprofen, diclofenac, methotrexate – and what did it do for ma chronic arthritis? Not a thing. Sure, they masked the pain for a while. Until I built up a tolerance. So their pushers, I mean my doctor, fed me more and more, stronger and stronger pills, until I became hooked and as numb as yer mouth after visiting the dentist. So yes, you're right, sonny, it's not ideal lining dope dealer's pockets. But at least they're honest about what they do.'

Ah'm stunned. The coppers look stunned. Even Kara looks sheepish for grassin on ma gran.

'Jean...' begins the copper. He looks serious. 'Does this stuff really work?'

'Sonny, the first night I took it, I had the best sleep of ma life. I woke up feeling like I did in my twenties. Before lunch, I had gutted the house, did the washing and ironing, I even hung they new curtains I'd bought years before. Since using this medicine I've been pain-free. It really has given me a new lease of life. Never thought I'd say this, but the sooner we follow the Yanks lead, the better.'

'And if we confiscate it?'

Her body slumps, n she gazes off intae the distance. 'I don't even want to *think* about what tonight will be like.'

The copper glances at his colleague who gives a slight nod. He screws the lid oan tight, n slips it intae gran's handbag. 'Did you say something about having a train to catch?'

'I did.' She zipps her bag shut n flashes him a big smile. 'Thanks, son. And apologies for giving you a hard time earlier.'

The police officer nods n returns the smile. 'No worries.' He turns n resumes his position at the top ay the stairs. 'Safe journey, and enjoy your soaps.'

We walk through the station in awkward silence n board our train. We sit across fae one another, n our eyes meet.

'Well,' ah say, 'at least ah know wit tae get you for Christmas.'

'Charles,' ma gran says quietly as she leans forward n looks me in the eye. 'If I *ever* catch you buying dope, I'll break every single one of your fingers. Understood?'

Ah nod. 'Got it.'

Gran sits back before striking up a conversation wae the woman across fae us aboot the weather.

Ah smile n look oot the winday. Turns oot gran's a bit of a bad ass.

THE CHOICE

Pearly gates or Dante's inferno
  Wispy clouds or rivers of fire
  Shimmering angels or shifting shadows
  Lines of scripture...or lines of coke
  Skinny salads or filling feasts
  Seventy-two virgins or two fire-breathing whores
  Wine with Michelangelo or absinthe with Van Gogh
  Melodic tunes plucked on golden harps, or soul-stealing riffs
strummed on Hendrix' guitar
  Stagnant comfort or struggling change
  Despondent despair or delightful debauchery
  Entropy or growth
  Boredom or revelry
  heaven or Hell
  The choice, is yours...

A poem, by S.A. Tan

THE FLYING SQUAD

I'm hanging onto the back window of this police car for dear life as it takes a hard left. PC Tunnok, she's in the front passenger seat, calling out muffled directions. PC Leahman, he's hammering it under blues and twos. The film crew in the back are doing their best to keep the camera stable and focused. On the plus side, it'll only add to the high-octane atmosphere when this segment airs. Assuming this shout is noteworthy, of course.

It's been almost three days I've been a fly-on-the-wall to the BBC Scotland crew filming a fly-on-the-wall cop show. However, they don't like being called the BBC anymore. That's what the cameraman told the cops on day one. Something about Pornhub ruining that acronym. And he's not a cameraman, he righteously informed the cops. That term is too problematic. It's 'camera-person' or 'camera-operator', although he prefers 'cinematographer and documentarian of real world occurrences'. I've named him SIMP – Self Important Marxist Prick.

SIMP's sound technician is sat next to him. I call her Rey, as like the *Star Wars* character she's instantly forgettable. I was a bit surprised that 'sound technician' is still okay, as that's very othering to the deaf—sorry, audibly impaired.

The two cops are an odd couple. Think of some of the most famous police-show double acts. Starsky and Hutch, Bodie and Doyle, Regan and Carter. Then think of the complete opposite. PC Leahman is...

mature? Experienced? Whatever the new name for someone formerly known as old is. Let's go with chronologically progressive. PC Leahman is a chronologically progressive English fellow. Or at least he looks it. He's probably still the right side of fifty, but his face is wrinklier than an elephant's ballsack, and he carries himself with all the vigour of a sackful of wet midgets. It's ironic having an Englishman enforce the diktats of a Scottish nationalist, state-run police force. Be like a black man working security at a BNP rally.

His partner, PC Tunnok, is a vertically challenged birthing-person with big bones who menstruates. She's very knowledgeable, our wee PC Tunnok, and loves nothing better than re-educating the dinosaur that is PC Leahman. Every time she opens her mouth and utters the words, 'Well *ack-chewally* it's...' or, 'That's *so* offensive...' I get the overwhelming urge to buzz to her mouth and lay some maggots. Together, they've come to be known as Cricket and Tubbsy. Together, they're enough to have the criminals and neds of Scotland's busiest and most notorious police division shaking in their boots. Too bad they're shaking with laughter.

Just this morning before setting out on patrol, SIMP was bemoaning the lack of decent footage. Sure, we've attended stabbings and beatings, gangland attacks and murders, robberies, arson, and overdoses. Plenty of overdoses. It seems this country is awash with synthetic opioids, but who cares about a junkie dying in a delicious pool of their own vomit? It's hardly worth a write-up in the local rag, never mind primetime viewing, and certainly not fitting of the narrative SIMP'S masters at the propaganda machine formerly known as the BBC are paying him to manufacture.

I've a good feeling about this one, though. All Tubbsy said after pressing her radio against her ear as we waited on an ambulance to turn up for yet another overdose victim was, 'We're needed elsewhere,' before winking at SIMP and adding, 'You'll want to keep the camera running for this one.'

So we left the young man looking like Harvey Dent with the amount of tasty vomit caked to one side of his face in the arms of his distraught mother, and raced to the cop car. Cricket hammered it away from that rundown tenement so hard, I had to work the two pulvilli on each of my six claws harder than a kid in a Chinese sweatshop to stick to the back window. SIMP and Rey couldn't get their seatbelts unwound enough to wrap it around themselves. Not that it matters. Cricket and Tubbsy show the same disdain for their own seatbelts as they did when attending that girl threatening to throw herself from the viaduct. Perhaps if she'd been a victim of online abuse rather than a jilted lover, they might have shown more enthusiasm and actually talked her down. On the bright side, her bloated corpse would have made prime larvae-laying-ground for some of my kin before they fished her from way downriver. Anyway, who needs seat belts when all the protection you could ever want comes from the cloth muzzles they all wear on their faces?

We careered through swathes of desolate schemes inhabited by hordes of dispossessed before Cricket calls out, 'This is it!' He slows and turns into the brand new housing development on the edge of town. 'We're looking for number thirty-two, Gaia Circus.'

'Gaia Circus is this way!' Tubbsy says, pointing a chunky finger towards the right.

Which is probably how she spends her time online. Bah-dum-tss!

Cricket floors it before slamming on the brakes and bouncing over the first speed-bump. They continue this neck-jarring cycle through this carbon copy of suburban utopia. Seems these bland, soulless estates are popping up all over former green-belts on the edges of civilisation. Not that I'm complaining. More bins means more food for me.

We turn onto Gaia Circus. Tubbsy, her eyes fixed out the front passenger window, calls out house numbers as she sees them. 'Two, four, six, eight'—her powers of detection are mighty great—'it must be further along this side.' Cricket flies over another two speed bumps before skidding to a halt outside number thirty-two.

There's a young woman sitting outside the house on the front doorstep. She has her legs pulled tight against her chest, her head buried between her knees, and is rocking back and forth, clearly distressed.

'Stay close to us,' Tubbsy says to the camera crew as she puts her cap on and reaches for the door handle. 'This could get ugly.'

I follow them as they all pile out, and fly towards the house, finding a good vantage point on the porch above the door. I gently land in case my weight causes this new build to come crumbling down. Fuck, even the three little pigs weren't stupid enough to build their houses from kits. And they certainly wouldn't have borrowed quarter-of-a-million quid for the privilege to live in them.

The young woman below me is peeking through her legs as the cops approach before burying her face and sobbing. Laughter and chattering comes from the rear of the house, as well as the irresistible scent of charcoal and cooking meat. Sounds like there's a party in full swing

'Ma'am,' begins Cricket before remembering with the help of a coughed, 'ahem' from Tubbsy. 'Forgive me. My name is PC Leahman, he/him, how can we help?'

The victim below lifts her head and theatrically wipes invisible tears from her cheeks with the back of her tattooed hand. Henceforth, she will be known as Scarlett Johansson, as with that level of acting she'll never win an Oscar.

'A-am I going t-to be on TV?' she says, glancing between the camera crew and cops.

'Only if you want to,' Tubbsy says. 'If you're not comfortable with it they can pixelate your fac—'

'No, no, it's fine,' Scarlett Johansson says, straightening her green hair and pulling her hammer-and-sickle muzzle up from her chin. 'My given name is Delilah, but am known by the name Storm-willow, zie/zim.'

Ah, for fuck sake, there's a surprise. How the hell did this species make it to the top? A nappy would be more appropriate than the muzzle she wears.

'Storm-willow, I am PC Tunnok'—wrong, you're Tubbsy—'she/her. Were you the one who called 999?'

Scarlett Johansson sniffles. 'I am.'

'Tell us, Storm-willow, what's happened?'

'It's...It's...' Scarlett Johansson gazes off into the distance.

'Everything's alright, Storm-willow,' Cricket says. 'You can tell u—'

'Everything is NOT alright,' snaps Scarlett Johansson, pulling her, I mean *zir* muzzle back down to zir chin. 'I have just been assaulted yet you have the gall to stand there mansplaining to me? Sheer fucking hubris.' She, sorry, *zie* buries zir head back into zir legs and wails like a wounded beached whale.

Poor Cricket's eyes look flustered at this vicious reaction to yet another unwitting faux pas.

Tubbsy gives him the evils before removing her cap and sitting on the doorstep next to Scarlett Johansson. She turns her radio down. I guess someone else can get that call from control about a mass brawl outside a pub not two miles from here.

'Apologies for my boomer partner,' Tubbsy says. 'He's still learning, but we'll get him there. Eventually. Now, how about you tell me exactly what's happened to you. Don't worry, this is a safe space.'

Scarlett Johansson lifts h—fuck, *zir* head and looks Tubbsy in the eyes, zir bottom lip quivering and fake lashes fluttering. 'It is?'

Tubbsy nods and appears to be smiling. 'We won't let anything bad happen to you. And if anyone tries.' She pulls her telescopic truncheon from her belt and extends it with a flick of the wrist. 'They'll be fishing bits of this out their backside for weeks.'

Scarlett Johansson's face cracks into something resembling a smile.

Sh—fuck, *zie* stretches zir legs out and wraps zir arms around zieself – mindlessly stroking the Chairman Mao tattoo on zir upper arm.

'It's...' begins Scarlett Johansson, '...my uncle.'

It's *always* the uncle.

'He...he...' zie bites zir pierced bottom-lip and shakes zir head.

'What did he do to you, Storm-Willow,' Tubbsy purrs in soft, soothing tones.

Scarlett Johansson wipes an invisible tear from zir eye. 'He assaulted me.'

Cricket shakes his head and says, 'For the love of Go—' Tubbsy shoots a cold hard glare at him. '—llum.'

'In what way,' asks Tubbsy, 'did your uncle assault you?'

Scarlett Johansson breaks the fourth wall by staring directly at the camera and saying, 'He hate-crimed me by telling an Englishman, Irishman, Scotsman joke.' Zie makes air quotes at the word joke.

'You, poor, poor thing,' Tubbsy says, squeezing Scarlett Johansson's shoulder before wrapping her arm around zir, showing the watching masses how empathetic Police Scotland are. Scarlett Johansson leans into Tubbsy and begins sobbing.

SIMP must be foaming at the zip at this. Not only does he have some hard-boiled crime-drama footage to present to his masters, it appears he may also have a budding romance subplot. It's apt we're on a street with circus in its name as all I see is comedic satire.

Less Shakespearean, more pantomime, Tubbsy gets in on the act and addresses the camera. 'This incident clearly shows the fact that words are violence.' —wait, I thought silence was violence— 'In accordance with the hate-crime act, that *joke* could be perceived as stirring up hatred against a protected group.'

'It could?' says Cricket.

I have a sneaky feeling that inside he wants to go all old school and urge his partner to be less Judge Dredd, and more Scales of Justice. Too bad his nuts are in a pouch hanging from Tubbsy's belt.

'Yes,' Tubbsy curtly states. 'Anything that can be interpreted as racist, sexist, classist, ageist, ableist, homophobic, biphobic, transphobic, xenophobic, Islamaphobic, anti-religion or anti-atheist is deemed hateful. Bottom line – this sort of speech is *not* good.'

'And anything deemed not good for you is bad, hence illegal,' mutters Cricket.

'Exactly,' Tubbsy says, the reference going above her polluted head. 'Let me guess, Storm-willow, the premise of the joke was either the Irishman being neuro-regressive and therefore appearing intellectually-challenged, or the Scotsman being fiscally conservative?'

Scarlett Johansson lifts her, no, *zir* head from the safe space that is Tubbsy's bosom. 'I don't know. I covered my ears and ran from there and called yourselves before the punchline'—more fucking air quotes—'was delivered.'

'Either way, it's xenophobic, and at the end of the day, it's as harmfully hateful as the day is long.'

'And what about using the term "man"?' Cricket sheepishly says. 'Surely it should be cisgender-man, should it not?'

Tubbsy, looking a wee bit stunned, slowly claps and nods and says, 'Clever boy. And here's me thinking re-education doesn't work.'

'And of course,' pipes up SIMP, not wanting left out of the baying mob, 'the fact everyone in the joke are cisgender-men – probably all white as well – is problematic in of itself. It's very exclusionary to not have representation of the other 348 genders and sexualities.'

'Storm-willow, was there any mention of their ethnicity?'

'No, but I interpreted them to all be white.'

Tubbsy and SIMP share a bewildered glance before shaking their heads and muttering, 'Structural white supremacy' at the same time.

'And I bet they all *walk* into a *bar* which is highly problematic and exclusionary to the differently-abled, and very triggering for people suffering from substance misuse issues.'

'Which in turn makes it even more racist due to the fact survivors of substance misuse are over-represented in marginalised, indigenous communities.'

'And I'm willing to bet that when they all walk into this bar, they ask something of the bar*man*.'

'More exclusionary language, as well as assuming this barperson's gender.'

Somebody sighs. Likely me. Don't ask me who said what in this radical progressive, woke circle-jerk. All I know is it's enough to give my arsehole a headache.

'The rap sheet is going to be lengthy on this one,' Tubbsy says. 'Storm-willow, is the perp still on the premises?'

Scarlett Johansson nods. 'He's round the back garden with the rest of my family.'

'He is?' Tubbsy bounces up from the step as quick as her frame allows. She's still gripping her fully-extended truncheon. 'Storm-willow, what's his name and can you describe him for me?'

'Of course I can. His name is Patrick, but everyone calls him Paddy. Which if you ask me'—nobody did—'is very racist.'

'One hundred percent agree. What does this Paddy look like?'

'He's short, I mean, he's around five-foot in height, with a big, flattened, red nose, strong Irish accent, and ginger hair.'

'Actually,' says SIMP, 'it's *red* hair.'

Tubbsy glares at SIMP. 'True, but that shows just how poisonous this speech is, and how it spreads like a virus, and how even victims aren't immune to it. A bit like Stockholm syndrome. Either way, this Paddy character must be stopped before he causes even more harm.' Tubbsy turns her radio back up and speaks over one of her old school colleagues, screaming for backup at the mass-brawl incident. Something about machetes and swords and ears being bitten off. She mumbles some police-code jargon into her mic before turning to Cricket. 'Ready to take down some bad guys?'

Guys? Tisk, tisk, tisk.

'Shouldn't we wait for back-up? We've no idea how many people are around there, and by the sounds of it, they've had more than a tipple.'

'We don't have time. This Paddy could be poisoning the minds of innocent people as we speak. It's our sworn duty to protect the vulnerable, and thanks to Dear Leader, what's said in the sanctity of the home is no longer a barrier to our just cause. I've requested a hate-crime patrol car and a safe-space ambulance to treat Storm-Willow, but god knows how many people this Paddy will have harmed with his hateful words by the time they get here. It's up to us, partner. If you aint with me, you're against me. Your choice.'

And with that, our intrepid upholders-of-the-law show little concern for their own safety, and make for the back garden of this crime infested, upper middle-class house, with SIMP and whatsername in tow.

I've seen enough and fly away to find some dog shit. Those doughnuts back in the police car aren't going to vomit over themselves.

TO MEND A BROKEN HEART

Colin's phone vibrates in his trembling hand.

'Crazy...I'm crazy, for feelin, so lone-ly...'

The screen reads, *'Private Caller'*, but he knows exactly who it is. He also knows they can't help. No one can. He presses the red icon, slides the device into his jeans pocket, steps onto the chair, and slips the rope over his head.

His phone vibrates against his leg – Patsy Cline's muffled tones still sounding beautiful.

Fuck knows why he'd changed his ringtone to that. Perhaps because it was his gran's favourite. At every family do, after she'd sunk a few brandies, she'd saddle up to the DJ and convince him to let her have a sing-song. They never refused. The moment that iconic piano intro sounded, everyone stopped what they were doing and turned to face her. She'd stand there, dressed in her sparkly black-dress with the big golden brooch, and belt out an emotion filled rendition that would have the great Patsy herself smiling down in appreciation.

His phone falls silent as he wonders what gran would make of this shit show.

She always had an answer for any problem. An answer that began with a bowl of her homemade soup – lentil, chicken, tomato, or his favourite – scotch broth.

'Gotten into trouble at School? Don't worry, son. My soup will make it all better.'

'Caught underage drinking again? Don't worry, son. My soup will make your tanned hide as right as rain.'

'Lost your licence for drunk driving? Don't worry, son. My soup's better than any fancy motor.'

'Lost the family savings gambling? Don't worry, son. Money comes, money goes, but a bowl of my homemade soup will always be here for you.'

Now that he thinks of it, she *never* offered any answers. She did listen, though, and by the time that bowl had been softened, all worries were gone. God, what he'd give for one more bowl of that soup.

He wipes the tears from his sodden cheeks and steels himself – all the listening in the world isn't going to fix this one. Action is what's required.

Standing on tiptoes, he tightens the noose – his pulse throbbing against the thick, coarse rope. Sweat streams down the inside of his arms, and his stomach churns. His short, sharp breaths grow louder, calling attention to themselves.

'Crazy...I'm crazy, for feelin, so lone-ly...'

Colin sighs. They're persistent but there's no point answering. His mind was made. He *had* to do this. He wished there was another way, but it was the only option. He hoped the call handlers wouldn't blame themselves.

Fuck!

What about the paramedics and police who'd find him? He hadn't even considered the impact finding his lifeless body swinging from the rafters might have on them.

Guilt rakes at his insides as he fishes his mobile from his pocket. He sends the call to voicemail and opens the text messenger – scans through the pre-prepared text with tear-filled eyes. This had been the most difficult message he'd ever had to compose.

He flinches when his phone vibrates to life, almost dropping it and worse – nearly falling from the chair.

He hits the red button.

His thumb hovers over the send text button.

The ticking clock on the wall reminds him that time isn't a luxury. They'd said it was only a matter of hours now.

He bites his lip and sends the message.

The moment the received notification pops up he drops his phone – it clatters onto the wooden floor of their summerhouse.

All preparation is done. Only one thing left.

'Crazy...'

Sirens wail in the distance, as if calling to him, begging him not to do it.

'I'm crazy, for feelin, so lone-ly...'

His blurry eyes fall upon the photo of his wife and daughter he'd tacked to the wall in front of him.

'I'm crazy...'

He takes one last deep breath.

'Crazy, for feelin, so blue...'

He exhales fully.

'I knew, you'd love me, as long, as you wanted...'

Standing on one foot, Colin kicks the chair away with the other.

'And then someday, you'd leave me, for some-body new...'

Adrenaline floods his body as the rope bites into his throat.

'Worry...'

The sirens get closer.

'Why, do I let myself, worry...'

Stars dance in his peripheral vision.

'Wondrin, what, in the world, did I do...'

An overwhelming sense of bliss sweeps over him as his vision narrows on the picture of all he loves in this world.

'Oh, crazy, for thinkin, that my love, could hold you...'
Colin's head lolls forward as his legs kick for the last time.
'I'm crazy for tryin, and cra-zy for cryin, and I'm crazy, for lo-vin, you...'

* * *

'Ding-a-ling-a-ding-dong.'

Louise jolts and lifts her head from her hand. The upbeat jingle of her phone in stark contrast to the hospital machines keeping her daughter alive. She lets go of her hand, being mindful not to catch any of the myriad of tubes and wires attached to Heather, and snatches her phone from the bedside cabinet.

This had better be Colin.

She grits her teeth and silently curses him. Of all the times to go AWOL. She'd sensed he was concealing something when he said he was nipping out to make a call, but never thought to question it. This better not be the old, 'Crazy Colin' starting to come back. Although he'd gotten his act together after Heather's diagnosis, and had been a rock throughout these last couple of hellish years, he really should be here, with his family, on what's likely the last hours of their daughter's life.

She unlocks her phone. At the top of the notification bar, above countless unread messages of sympathy and support, is a message from Colin. She opens it immediately.

Louise, I want you to know, I love you and Heather more than life itself. That's why I'm doing this. It's the only way she'll get a new heart in time.

I've called the police and ambulance and told them where they can find my body. I need you to make sure my heart goes to our daughter. I've instructed a solicitor to come to you at the hospital with the relevant donor forms. He'll help you deal with the authorities. I'm so sorry to leave you like this but it's the only way. You're a wonderful mother and the best wife a man could ever hope for. I know you'll do a grand job raising Heather, and if she becomes half the person you are, then I'll be a proud dad. Kiss her every day for me. I love you both. Goodbye. x x x

Louise springs to her feet, sends the chair clattering over. Her legs almost buckle at the knees, and it's as though a horse has just booted her in the stomach.

Her thumb hovers over '*Call Hubby*' as her eyes dart between Heather and her phone. She dismisses the thought and presses the button, willing it to hurry up and connect.

The ringing tone sounds.

She paces the room as tears stream down her face, pleading, begging, for him to answer.

What the fuck is he thinking? Heather had fought this like a Trojan, outlasting the most positive of doctor's opinions, and Louise hoped her daughter still had another round or two left in her.

'No!' she cries as Colin's voicemail instructs her to leave a message.

She hangs up and tries again. This time, the sound of her husband's voicemail is joined by an equally horrific sound – a continuous beep from Heather's heart monitor.

'No! Please God, help me,' she begs, knowing no help – divine or otherwise – is coming.

Why had she been so *stupid* as to authorise a do not resuscitate clause for Heather?

She stumbles towards her dying daughter and collapses at the side of her bed. She drops her phone, takes Heather's hand in hers, and wails at the top of her lungs – cursing every god under the sun.

She pulls herself to her feet, and gazes upon Heather's angelic face as she strokes it and sobs uncontrollably.

She kisses her. 'I–I love you *so* much, Heather.' She kisses her again. 'S–s–so does your d–dad. You t–two look out for each other.' She smiles. 'And behave. I don't want to be the talk of the steamy by the time I... get...' Louise lifts her head as her eyes drift skyward. '...up...there...'

The thought makes her feel all warm inside, and surprisingly, calm.

She kisses Heather and caresses her cheek with the back of her fingers. 'I'll see you soon, sweetie.'

She turns and trudges to the far side of the room.

The bustling city floods the room as she opens the window.

She swings a leg out the window, glances over her shoulder for one last look at her daughter, before falling to join her family.

THE GIFT THAT KEEPS ON GIVING

Lashing rain floods my taxi's windscreen faster than the wipers can clear it, and the headlights aren't much better than useless. On a quiet country-road I'd normally take faster than Muhammad Ali getting into bed at night, I'm crawling along like a pensioner on Valium. Even that feels too fast.

The dashboard clock gives me some good news – any hires from now will be charged at double rate.

A cigarette-roughened voice crackles over the radio. 'Merry Christmas, Bill.'

I key the mic. 'Same to you, Julie.'

'Are you free?'

'Yep,' I say, hoping there's another hire. 'Dropped the punter off ten minutes ago.'

'Doubt you'll get any more tonight.'

'Yeah, unlikely,' I say, hoping she's wrong. 'I'll hang about for a bit when I get back. Just in case.'

'How far away are you?'

'Further than I'd like to be in this weather.'

'Any snow where you are?'

'Possibly,' I say, 'although I can't see it for all the rain.'

'Typical. My Dylan went to bed dreaming of a white Christmas. Think he's more excited for snow than he is for Santa. Bloody weather forecasters.'

I laugh. 'I'd hang the lot of them. Them and traffic wardens.'

'What about the taxman?' she says between coarse laughs. 'Is there room on your gallows for him?'

'My gallows are big enough for all the wankers of the world. Including, but not restricted to, bankers, politicians, learner drivers, used car salesmen, and suicide bombers.'

'What about old ladies with shopping trolleys that walk in front of you slower than a week in jail?'

'Hoi,' I say, feigning insult. 'My mum's one of them.'

There's a moments silence. 'Sorry, Bill, but she's got to go.'

'Fair enough. At least I'll get a shit-load of cash from selling her house. Every cloud and all that.'

'Oh! You're a bad boy, William McClelland. It's safe to say Santa won't be coming down your chimney tonight.'

'If he does, he's onto plums. Literally. Adele's on that vegan diet so there's not a mince pie to be had at mine. Less and less meat gets bought at each shop. Think she's trying to convert me.'

'Get her on your gallows before it's too late!'

'Nah, think she'd just eat her way through the rope. It's got to taste better than the crap she's eating. Would need to be the firing squad for her and her vegan comrades.'

'I'll need to tell her that next time I run into her.'

'Do that and I'll tell Dylan that Santa Claus isn't real.'

'I think he'll come to that conclusion when he wakes to a snowless Christmas.'

'Nah,' I say as I round a sharp bend. 'There's time yet. It might—'

My headlights illuminate something on the road. I drop the mic, slam on the brakes, and grip the wheel with both hands as I swerve into the middle of the road. My taxi wiggles to a stop as my heart pounds against my ribcage, sending adrenaline surging through my body.

What the fuck was that?

My eyes dart between the mirrors. Seeing nothing, I turn and peer out the rear windscreen.

'You there, Bill?'

I turn on the hazard lights and reach into the passenger footwell for the mic. I take a deep breath and key it.

'Eh, yeah,' I say. 'I almost hit...something on the road.'

'Are you okay?' she says, the concern clear in her voice.

'I'm fine,' I lie.

'What was it?'

'I'm not sure. It looked like a person, but I only caught a glimpse and I can't see anything from here. I'm going to check it out. Standby.'

I slot the mic into its holder, reach underneath my seat, and pull out the heavy torch I keep there in case of emergencies.

'Oooh...' Julie says, sounding croakier than usual. 'Might be the ghost of Christmas past.'

I smile but inside I'm shitting myself. I pull my hood up and open the door – the wind almost rips the handle from my grasp. I step out and feel soaked to the bone before I even get the door shut. I turn the torch on and point it back the way I came – raindrops fall like missiles.

'Hello?' I call.

Nothing.

I walk to the back of my taxi and sweep the beam from left to right.

'Is anybody there?'

Still nothing.

The wind picks up, buffeting me, driving the rain into my face, and blowing my hood down. I dip my head and fumble with both hands at it. I manage to pull it tight around my head, and with the torch still facing skyward, I glance up.

A silhouette stands along the road.

'Hello,' I call out again, sounding meek.

No reply comes.

Part of me wants to shine the beam of light at it, while another part – the part that remembers every horror film I'd seen – is screaming to get back in my taxi and take off.

I slowly lower the torch. The light reveals a woman stood with her head bowed and face concealed behind long, black, matted hair.

She looks up, squinting at the bright light. I nearly run when she lifts her hand to shield her eyes.

'Can you help me?' she says, in a normal, un-ghost-like voice.

'Yes,' I say, as my shoulders relax.

I switch off the torch and – keeping a firm grasp of it, just in case – walk towards her.

I reach her and stop. She's wearing a retro, white and blue-floral dress, white tights, and blue platform heels. She's absolutely drenched. Wetter than Whitney Houston's last joint, as my pal Malky would say.

'Are you okay?' I say.

She looks at me and nods. Her face is emotionless – cold, even.

'What you doing out here?'

'Christmas present,' she says, as if that was enough explanation.

'Where's your car?'

'Car?' she says, glancing around the ground as if she'll find it lying at her feet.

I switch on the torch and sweep it along the roadside, revealing nothing but skeletal trees, and threadbare hedges. A river or stream burbles somewhere beyond the hedgerow.

'Where do you live?'

She looks at me, confused. 'Live?'

'Yes, where's your home?'

'Home?'

Jesus, Mary, Joseph and the wee donkey. She's either a no-righter or in shock. Not that I had any experience with people in shock. I'm just going by how they act in the films.

'Yes,' I say, 'home. It's a building filled with people who annoy the life out of you. Sometimes known as family.'

'Yes,' she says, her eyes lighting up. 'Family. Home. Can you take me?'

'Of course I can,' I say before the voice of doubt can dissuade me.

I turn to head back to my taxi – she doesn't move.

'Look.' I shine the light on my taxi. 'I'm a taxi driver, there's no need to be afraid. Come, let's get out of this weather.'

She slowly follows me looking dazed and confused.

I open the rear, passenger-side door for her, and she steps in. I close the door and walk to the boot, open it and grab the towel and tartan blanket I keep in there, giving my face and hands a quick dry. I get in the driver's seat and turn the heater up full.

'Here,' I say, passing the towel and blanket to the drenched lady in the backseat. 'Get yourself warm and dry. You're wetter than an otter's pocket.'

She takes them without so much as a flicker of emotion. Should've went with the Whitney Houston line.

I turn and start up the sat-nav. 'So, where to?' I say, looking at her through the rear-view mirror.

'Home,' she says, staring out the side window.

'You'll have to be more specific. Does "home" have a name?'

'Yes,' she says, without breaking her vigil from the window.

This human riddle is starting to piss me off. 'What's it called then?'

'Burnsbridge Farm.'

At last, we're getting somewhere. I type the address into the sat-nav, half expecting it to come up blank. It doesn't. The sat-nav informs me it's just under five miles from my current location – a ten-minute drive. Something tells me the weather and chatterbox of fun in the back seat will make this drive feel much longer. I inform Julie of my detour, and set off for Burnsbridge Farm.

We drive in silence. My eyes keep drifting to the rear-view mirror, sneaking peeks at the strange woman behind me. She's pretty, in a sort of hippie-chick way, and looks to be around thirty. Her skin is pale, and lips seem to have a bluish tinge to them. She has a distant sort of detached demeanour, and she smells like a wet dog and...well, something I can't quite place.

'In three-hundred yards, turn left,' says the soothing voice of the sat-nav.

I indicate, slow down, and lean forward, peering out the window. There's no signs warning of a turn ahead, and I struggle to see it.

'Turn left.'

I catch sight of a turning. Actually, it's more like a gap in the hedges. I turn into it and am on a single track, rutted dirt-road. The steering lightens and wheels spin on the muddy surface. Tall overgrown hedges press in on either side. The longer branches reach out like gnarled limbs and scrape along the side of my taxi.

My jaw clenches. See if I get stuck or my taxi damaged.

'In two-hundred yards, you will arrive at your destination.'

We bounce and slide along the final two hundred yards until a gap appears in the hedgerow. I turn onto a gravel driveway lined with a rotted wooden fence. After thirty yards, the driveway opens up to a courtyard surrounded by farm buildings. The far side is alive with flashing Christmas-lights from the farmhouse.

'Home sweet ho—'

My taxi's interior light comes on. I glance over my shoulder in time to see the door close. Darkness fills my taxi once more. The woman heads for the house like a moth to a flame. She disappears around the side without so much as a wave of thanks.

I sigh and shake my head. There's gratitude for you.

The motor of the rear windscreen wiper drones to life as I shift into reverse. Wrapping my arm around the passenger seat, I turn to look out the rear window, knowing I won't see a thing. Only I do. There, on the back-seat, is a box. I knock the gear stick out of reverse, put the handbrake on, stretch over, and grab the box with one hand.

I turn on the interior light. The brightly decorated cube with a smiling clown on the front, and red handle on the side tells me it's a jack-in-the-box. I scratch my head as my mind casts back to my encounter with the strange lady by the roadside. I don't recall her carrying this, and I'm sure it wasn't left by my last hire either as he'd sat in the front. The voice of doubt urges me to toss it out the window – my good deed for the day is done.

But it is Christmas...

I sigh and curse to myself before opening the door and stepping into the wild weather again. Forcing the door closed, I begin for the house before stopping – the house is in complete darkness.

What the...?

The wee voice that's seen far too many scary movies pipes up again. I silence it and begin for the house, if only to get out of this weather.

I round the farmhouse and the wind eases up, creating an eerie silence interspersed with the crunch of gravel underfoot. I'm bathed in light when a motion sensing flood-light turns on. An ugly, wooden-clad porch juts from the traditional stone-built house.

I reach the porch and my hand hovers over the doorbell. I should probably just leave the jack-in-a-box by the door, but curiosity gets the better of me. I ring the bell and am answered by muffled barking from inside.

A light goes on in an upper floor window. The barking gets clearer. I step back as the porch light comes on. The door opens and two Rottweilers led by a Jack Russel bound into the porch. I step back further as an elderly lady dressed in a white housecoat opens the door to the porch. All three dogs stream from the door and head straight for me.

I freeze as the two big dogs circle me while the smaller one yaps and jumps at me. My arse is making buttons and I'm holding my breath, praying the two Rotties don't decide to show the same aggro as the wee yap acting like it's a lion.

'Genghis!' shouts the old woman. 'Leave him be.'

The small dog glances at the old woman before scurrying away for more pressing matters. The two bigger dogs follow. Genghis's eyes remain locked on me as it cocks its leg against the building.

'Don't mind them,' says the old woman. 'Genghis has some trust issues, so he can be a bit antisocial at times.'

'At least he's living up to his name,' I say, forcing a nervous smile.

The old woman's face remains blank as she crosses her arms. She's staring at the toy in my hands.

'Sorry to bother you,' I continue, 'but I've just—'

'Dropped a young woman off?'

'—eh...Yes. She's left a—'

'Jack-in-the-box in your car?'

'—um...yes, can you give her it?' I say, as I stretch my arm towards her.

She backs away and shakes her head. 'I'm afraid I can't.'

'Why not?'

'Because she's dead.'

It takes a moment for her comment to sink in. 'Pull the next one. I just dropped her off two minutes ago.'

She glances to the heavens as she tightens the belt on her housecoat. 'You won't believe me, but the woman you dropped off is'—she bites her lip—'was, my mother.'

The horror-film-loving voice takes great pleasure at this validation. I'm not convinced. 'I think you must be mistaken. The woman I dropped off was no more than thirty. So, either she knows the best plastic surgeon there is, or you've had the worst paper run in history.'

Her brow furrows and eyes narrow. 'Turn the handle.'

'Why?'

'Just indulge an old lady who's had a hard paper run.'

I smile as the horror-film-loving voice leaps from its high horse and continues its frenzied warnings.

'Okay,' I say, taking hold of the handle.

The familiar children's rhyme 'Pop Goes the Weasel' chimes from the toy as I slowly crank it.

'Christmas Eve of 1968,' She says, gazing above my head and into the distance. 'I was a girl of six, and wanted nothing more than a jack-in-the-box from Santa.'

Melodic tones emanate from the toy.

'Problem was,' she continues, 'I never told my parents until Christmas-Eve morning. I remember mother telling me that it was too late, that Santa had already checked his list, made his toys, and would already be packing them into his sack. There was nothing she could do. She told me that if I was good, I might get one for my birthday.'

The tune comes quicker as I turn the handle faster.

'Here's the problem with being an only child – you're used to getting what you want. I cried and pleaded, screamed and begged, until I broke my mother.' She sighs and shakes her head slightly. 'Tired of my crying, mother set out late in the afternoon on that Christmas eve – when the weather was similar to this – to try and find one of *those* toys for her spoiled daughter.' She closes her eyes and bites her lip. 'She never returned.'

I turn the handle faster yet, keeping time with my quickening heart.

'They found her car the next day, five miles along the road, upturned in the burn. The police said the crash hadn't killed her...she'd drowned.' She opens her now watery eyes. 'Every year since then those things'— she nods at the toy in my hands—'have appeared on Christmas morning. Sometimes we find them by the door. Other times we find them along the driveway. At first, we thought it was someone playing a sick joke. Until we found one in the house. It wasn't until the first passing motorist delivered one that we finally admitted something more sinister was going on.'

'Sinister?' I say, not quite believing this fantastical story. 'Doesn't it mean she loves you dearly if she keeps on bringing the toy you wanted?'

Her eyes meet mine. 'That's a...*nice* thought. Wrong, but nice all the same.'

A puzzled look must've crossed my face.

'You'll see,' she says.

'I'll see wha—'

A broken and mangled jack pops from its box with a blood-curdling scream, a screech of tyres, and smash of metal and glass. I almost jump out of my skin and drop the toy, recoiling like it's a live hand grenade.

'What the fuck was that?' I say.

'That,' she says quietly, 'is a mother's taunt, and a daughter's torment.'

Genghis marches over with his tail held high and inspects the toy lying at my feet.

The old lady makes a clicking sound and says, 'Come.'

Genghis goes into the house followed by his two big pals.

'Safe journey home,' she says, as she closes the door. 'And merry Christmas.'

The porch light goes off, leaving me in darkness. I stride from the door and wave my hands in the air until the floodlight comes on. I speed walk back to my taxi, constantly checking over my shoulder. I reach my taxi and look in the window before opening the door. Apart from the towel, blanket, and wet patch on the back seat, it's empty.

I'm gripping the steering wheel tight as I leave the courtyard, and don't relax a little until I'm back on the main road. I race from that place faster than I should be in this weather, especially with my attention spending more time checking the mirrors than on the road ahead.

By the time the tops of the high flats and churches of my town come into view, I've managed to pull my panicked mind from terrible thoughts. It's got to be some sort of prank they played on me, right?

Some music might distract me. I switch the stereo on, but get nothing but static noise. Must still be too far from home to receive a signal from the local radio station. I hit the auto scan button. The stereo runs through the bandwidth without picking up a signal.

That's odd.

I switch to the high frequency 'FM' band. The digits on the stereo whizz through their cycle without tuning to any of the national stations.

The weather must have knocked out a nearby mast.

It finally stops on a frequency I don't recognise – 2412.68. Faint music buried under a hail of static interference.

I turn the volume up, straining to hear the melody.

It doesn't sound like pop or rock, more...melodic. Perhaps I've tuned into *Classical FM.* Just my fucking luck.

I turn it up some more and freeze.

What the...

I'm straining to hear the tune over my quickened pulse, pounding against my eardrums. It sounds like...it sounds like...like...the all too familiar children's rhyme, 'Pop Goes the Wea'—

A wet hand touches my shoulder, sending my heart to my throat and my stomach to my arse. I flinch and involuntarily yank down on the steering wheel.

The last thing I see as my taxi hits the grass verge and takes off through the hedges, is the face of the young lady by the road, glaring at me through the rear-view mirror.

Only her face is no longer emotionless. It's contorted into what I can only describe as pure evil, while her eyes drip with hatred and malevolence.

Her blackened lips curl into a sneer, revealing rotted, broken teeth. 'Merry Christmas,' she growls.

JULIE ANDREWS KNOWS BEST

Imagine being cocooned in the womb while God, Allah, Zeus – witever ye want tae call the cunt – hugs ye tight. That's wit it's like, know wit ah mean. It's joost a travesty it never lasts.

That wis as big a hit as ah've ever took, but awready ah can feel the auld Devil cunt grabbin et us. He's tryin tae pull us fae this bliss, back tae cauld, harsh reality. It's joost a dull throbbin inside the noo. Soon, it'll be absolutely torcherous.

Ah'm becomin mair n mair aware ay ma surroundins. The cauld emptiness ay ma pokey wee flat. Ma deep breaths borderin oan snorin. The rancid smell like somehin's crawled in here n died. Ma numb arse fae the stiff flairboards. The kink in ma neck. The needle stickin intae the inside ay ma skinny thigh. The cauld emptiness ay ma pokey wee heart.

Shoulda joost jagged the whole fuckin lot.

These fuckin needles huv goat a lot tae answer fur, know wit ah mean. They've hud as big a bearin as can be oan ma life. They're the reason ah'm in this mess – this fuckin nightmare. Apparently, ma maw n da moved here fae the city cos ay these fuckin things.

The story goes, that when ah wis a toddler, ma maw wis walkin hame fae the shops wae me beside her. When we reached oor tenement, ah let go ay her hawn, n ran aheed up the close. Ma maw says ah tripped n fell, skiting heed first alang the concrete. She immediately ran tae us.

Wit she saw as she picked us up struck the fear ay god intae her. There, lyin right next tae where ah'd fell, wis a dirty needle. That wis plenty. That night when ma da goat in fae work, she laid doon the law. She telt him wit happened, n that this city isnae a good place tae be bringin up weans.

This wis the time when the dark spectre ay smack first reared its ugly heed in this country, know wit ah mean. The city wis hit hard. The brown plague infected whole swathes ay schemes. No tae mention wit it done tae inflame an awready violent gang culture. God knows how she done it, as ma da wis a city boy through an through, but before long we were flittin doon tae this quaint little seaside toon.

Ah sometimes wonder how they felt as they drove the big box-van packed wae aw oor stuff doon the motorway. Ah like tae imagine thum bein aw giddy an that. The excitement fur their new life away fae the shite ay the city coursin through thum like Afghanistan's finest. Ah can picture thum yappin away in the front while ah slept in the back. Plannin their new life the gither. Sharing their hopes, dreams, n aspirations fur me n the wee brother ah'd soon huv, wrapped up safe n sound in ma maw's womb.

Their ambitions never lasted long.

Ah can attest tae that, awright.

Ah slowly bring ma heed back up level, n stretch oot the kink. Ah rub ma hawns ower ma face n through ma greasy hair as the dull throb builds intae a poundin ache. Imagine havin a migraine in yer full body, while gettin telt that yer favourite granda – the wan that always takes ye fur a kickaboot doon the park – has joost died in a car crash wae yer dug, cat, hamster n goldfish. That doesnae even *begin* tae describe how ah'm feelin the noo. How ah'm *always* feelin withoot ma daily spoonful ay soothin, brown sugar.

Before the last box wis even unpacked, ma maw an da were dealt a soberin blow. The very first time ma maw went tae the wee newsagents at the tap ay oor street, a headline in the local rag caught her eye, n sunk her heart. It read: PRIEST ROBBED AT NEEDLE-POINT IN CHURCH BY JUNKIES.

Ma da went aff ees nut n aw that, havin a go at ma maw fur bringin us tae a place where folk were low enough tae rob priests in a fuckin church.

Ah often wonder how many faimily's ah've convinced tae "move somewhere better" wae the amount ay dirty needles ah've discarded over the years. Fuck, the mere sight ay me trawlin the streets like a zombie wid be enough tae send most sensible folk fleein, know wit ah mean.

If that hus happened, ah sincerely hope they've escaped fae aw this pish. Joost don't hawd yer breath. It's clear tae me, ye can *never* run fast enough, far enough, or long enough, tae escape yer demons. Thirs only wan way ah know, know wit ah mean.

Ah pull the needle ootay ma leg, unwrap the tinfoil, n setup ma spoon.

Here ah come, big man. Here. Ah. Come.

THE SPORTSMAN

This is it. The greatest achievement of Richard Johnson's life is here. The silver medalist beside him steps onto the podium to a rousing cheer.

Richard takes a deep breath to calm the nervous-energy coursing through his body.

Emotional roller-coaster doesn't even *begin* describing these last two years. With the sacrifices he'd made to reach this pinnacle, emotional turbulence was always guaranteed. Not that he hadn't made sacrifices before. No matter what they might say about him, they couldn't accuse him of lacking dedication to the sport. He'd devoted his entire childhood and teenage years in pursuit of this goal, but failed to make any impact. He was going nowhere.

That was before the change. One he had to make if he was to have any chance of making his dreams a reality. It was a change of mind, body and soul, a change for the better – a change forever.

Not everyone approves.

Although some might say he doesn't deserve this accolade, no one could say he hadn't worked his balls off to get here.

Still, there weren't many brave enough to call him out. Fear of being tarnished a bigot keeps the naysayers gagged.

'*And now,*' calls the stadium announcer. '*Representing the United Kingdom of Great Britain and Northern Ireland*' —Richard bites his quivering bottom lip—'*the new, record breaking*'—his eyes well and hands tremble—'*women's, triple-jump champion of the world*'—that breaks him, and the tears flow—'*Rachel Johnson!*'

Richard holds his chiselled jaw high as he steps onto the winner's podium to a spattering of applause.

THE STOREROOM

'Anyone craving bacon?' I say, breaking the taut silence shrouding our fire engine like noxious fumes.

Disgusted head shakes and shameful sniggering answer me.

'You had to go there, didn't you?' says the gaffer from the front seat. 'Kinda.'

'That was somebody's wee boy.'

'It was...now it's more like a Guy Fawkes dummy after bonfire night.'

That breaks them. Laughter fills the cab, eases the tension. It's the sorta laughing you do when you know it's so wrong, but at the same time, it's so right. And a good laugh is precisely what we all need right now.

'Too fucking far,' says the gaffer as we pull into the station.

'Man,' says James as he grabs his soot-stained helmet, and steps off the engine. 'You're so dark, the Devil's shitting himself waiting for your arrival.'

We disembark, close the bay-door, and get to work. Wet and contaminated fire kits need changing and sent for cleaning. Depleted breathing apparatus cylinders need replenishing, and reports must be written before we're ready for the next shout.

'Don't forget,' calls the gaffer, 'the burn dressings and oxygen cylinder need replacing.' He steps into his office and closes the door.

'I'll do it,' I say, thankful for the opportunity.

I enter the storeroom, close the door, slump against it, and burst into tears as the emotions hit me like a backdraught. I bite my lip and close my eyes. Big mistake.

A vision of the two parents, covered in burn dressings and sucking medical oxygen, surfaces in my mind. The whites of their wide-open eyes in stark contrast to their blackened faces, staring at the ambulance where the charred remains of their son lies.

There are things in this world no one should see. Things that leave scars so deep, not even the sands of time will fully heal.

I dry my eyes with a trembling hand while the other fumbles around in my pocket. I pull my phone out. The screensaver of my wife and son almost breaks me again. I take a deep breath and press 'Call Wifey'.

Two rings later, Lynne's sleepy but concerned voice answers. 'Ryan, what's wrong?'

'Nothing,' I lie.

'Then why call at this hour?'

'Eh...I just wanted to hear your voice.'

She's not buying it. 'Ryan,' she says softly, 'what's happened?'

I instinctively rub my upper lip as if to bar any revealing words that might slip out.

How I want to tell her about the horrific incident. About how I carried that lifeless toddler from that hellscape as his skin slipped from bone. How it took three burly firefighters to hold his screaming mother back from the flames. How her piercing wails struck at my very core. How the guilt clawed at my inside when all I could think of was my own wife and son, safely tucked up in bed at home. How the sheer thought of this happening to them terrifies me more than any raging inferno ever could.

But I don't.

I can't.

It's not her burden to bear.

'Is the wee man okay?' I say.

'Yeah, he's fine. He's sound asleep. Like I was.'

'Sorry.'

'Don't be, I'm fucking with you.'

I laugh. 'Will you do me a favour and check the smoke alarms?'

She sighs. 'Ryan, it's late, it'll waken Tyler.'

'Don't test them, just check the LEDs are blinking.'

She goes silent for a few moments before saying, 'Okay, I need a pee anyway.'

'Thanks,' I say as my shoulders relax. 'And Lynne...?'

'Yes?'

'Will you kiss the wee man for me?'

'Of course I will. Love you.'

'Love you too. G'night.'

I hang up, gather the required stock, and leave the storeroom feeling lighter than when I went in. Ready for the next shout.

LADS ON TOUR

The first time your child goes abroad is a time filled with worry and questions.

Does he have everything he needs?

Is he with good lads who'll look out for him?

Will he do the same for them?

Have we as parents prepared him to face the big bad world on his own?

He still looks like a wee boy. Tall for sixteen, but skinny, and never having shaved more than the fluff from his top lip.

His mother wraps her arms around him, squeezing tightly and planting kiss after kiss on his cheek.

'Mum,' he says, glancing around awkwardly.

'You be good,' she says, trying to sound firm. 'And keep out of trouble.'

'Mum,' he says, shaking his head.

'Aww, look at him,' she says, her bottom lip quivering. 'He's a man, sure enough.' She pinches his cheek.

'MUM!'

God, please don't let those words be his last.

He turns to me. How my heart yearns to do as his mother did.

I hold out a hand.

He takes it firmly and shakes it – a man's handshake.

I hold on longer than normal and look him in the eye.

'Just...' I say, struggling for the right words.

'Just...' My voice is strained and weak.

'Just...come home.'

He nods, lets go of my hand, straightens his Glengarry proudly sitting atop his head, swings his bergan over his shoulder, and boards the troopship.

His mother breaks down beside me, sobbing uncontrollably.

I wrap my arm around her and pull her in close.

A single tear sails down my cheek as my son sails off to war.

WHEN SKELETONS ESCAPE THE CLOSET

'Jonathan Simpson?' someone says in an official tone.

Ma attention shifts from the engrossing novel on ma phone's e-reader at the mention of ma name.

Wit the fuck is this?

A burly, middle-aged man, wearing a navy puffer-jacket and baseball cap, blocks the exit from the bus shelter. His bushy eyebrows are in the shape of a V, and a stern expression creases his hard, unshaven face. He holds a phone before him, the camera light shining. Five others stand behind him.

'You filming me?' I say.

'Answering a question wae a question implies dishonesty. Now, I'll ask again, are you Jonathan Simpson?'

I sigh and roll ma eyes. 'Mate—'

'Let's get one thing straight,' he spits, 'I'm no yer *mate.*'

'Is that right?'

He nods as his lips curl into a condescending smirk.

I know exactly how to deal with this clown. I look back at ma phone, trying to appear unfazed, but ma attention's firmly fixed on the gorilla and his gang barring ma only route outta this bus shelter.

'Well?' he says.

'Piss off,' I say. 'I'm no interested.'

'Naw,' comes a voice as shrill as a dentist's drill. 'We'll no be pissin off anywhere. No until you've answered our questions, ya animal.'

I close ma eyes, take a deep breath, and blow out hard through pursed lips. Ma heart's galloping, sending adrenaline coursing through ma body. I guess we're doing this then. I lock ma phone, slip it into ma pocket, and stand.

A peroxide-blonde woman with black roots stands behind the gorilla, peering over his shoulder. The I-want-to-speak-to-the-manager sneer on her make-up plastered face reveals teeth like a row of condemned houses, and she's skinnier than a bulimic junkie.

I lock eyes with the big man. 'Wit dae ye want?'

'We want tae know yer name,' Gorilla says.

'And why yer here,' Bulimic Junkie adds.

'I'm the tooth fairy,' I say, deadpan and keeping eye contact with Gorilla. 'And I'm here tae tell your bird she's bleedin me dry.'

'*Funny*,' she says, the offence clear in her voice. 'We'll see how much yer laughin when everyone finds out yer here tae meet a thirteen-year old for sex.'

I stammer with ma mouth open before it dawns.

'Very good,' I say, slowly clapping. 'You almost had me there. Who put yous up to this?'

'Jonathan,' she says, 'this isnae a joke. This is a serious offence with serious consequences. Ones you'll need tae face when the police arrive.'

I shake ma head and laugh. 'You're gonny have to try *much* harder to catch me out. So, who was it then? Bairdy? Yilmaz? No, I bet it was Farrer. This is something he'd do. Whoever it was, ye can tell them I'll get them back. *Big* time.'

The two share a glance before the woman pulls a pile of paper from her jacket. She holds a sheet up in front of me. 'This is you, right?'

It is. There's no denying it. It's a photo of me sunbathing on a Tenerife beach. Ma mind races. I've never seen this picture before, and for the life of me, can't work out how this woman has it.

'Where did you get that?' I say.

'From you.'

'Eh?'

'Don't play dumb, Jonathan, you sent it tae me in the chat room. Or should I say, you sent it to Amanda.' She makes air quotes at the name Amanda before shuffling through the pile of paper. 'We've also got a printout of every conversation you had with Amanda – who you believed was thirteen – including all the times ye asked to see her breasts, what you were going tae do to her when yous met, wh—'

She looks serious. They all do. This is either the best prank ever or... well, I'm no sure *what* the alternative could be. Ma eyes drift from the reams of paper as I lift ma head, trying to figure out what's going on. A small crowd's gathered, with some asking the question, 'Is he a paedo?' This is getting out of hand – way beyond a joke.

Then, the penny finally drops.

The moment *she* slowly drives past, the realisation hits me like a shovel to the head. This is the first time I've set eyes upon that poisonous cunt since we broke up. The smirk on her lips, and malice in her eyes tells me *she's* behind this.

She, being Chantelle.

You cold hearted, conniving bitch.

I go light-headed and am sure the mob sees the colour drain from ma face. Not that I'd notice. Their chattering accusations fade as the last venom Chantelle spat at me swirls around ma mind like a drunk on a bouncy castle.

'You'll regret leaving me,' she'd warned. 'I'll make sure of it.'

LOST IN TRANSLATION

Huh. I never even *knowed* bears wore rings. I don't think they'd be shiny ones with big diamonds, but they'd still be pretty. I think they would be made from twigs and berries.

I break a small, bendy branch from the big tree daddy climbed, and wrap it around my finger.

Yay! Daddy's coming back down.

'Did you find any bear-rings, Daddy?'

'No, Sweetie. I couldn't find our bearings.'

'Look! I've made one. We can give it to the big bear that was at our tent.'

Daddy picks me up and starts running through the forest again. He looks very scared. Maybe because it's nearly night-time, but I never even knowed daddy was scared of the dark.

'Is mummy still wrestling with the big bear?'

'Yes, sweetie. Mummy's still wrestling the bear.'

I kiss him and hug him. 'I love you...*and* mummy.'

Daddy cries again.

HOME OR HELL

Judith Boyd's first voyage aboard a ship at sea was not a pleasant one. Salt stung her lips and it was as though the Devil himself raked her guts. The previous day had been filled with so many joys of life, Judith felt blessed to be alive. Now, as she lay bound and helpless in the captains quarters, she prayed the Good Lord would come for her to end this torture.

She shifted her weight onto her other side as much as the thick, coarse rope binding her hands to the bedpost would allow – wincing as her hip dug into the firm boards of the tiny bed. Her own bed back at the castle was fit for neither king nor queen, but God, what she'd give to be tucked up in it. If only to be rid of the smell. What filling there was in this bed smelt like it had come straight from the stables. She shuddered to think of the amount of beasties infesting this poor excuse for bedding.

Judith jolted as a drum pounded above. This time the sole chanter asked a new question of the drunken crew.

> *'What shall we do wi the Virgin Mary?*
> *What shall we do wi the Virgin Mary?*
> *What shall we do wi the Virgin Mary?*
> *Erlie in the mornin!'*

The crew sung back as one.

> *'Whey-hey, an up she rises,*
> *Whey-hey, an up she rises,*
> *Whey-hey, an up she rises,*
> *Erlie in the mornin!'*

A different crewman from the first offered his suggestion.

> *'We'll...tak her below an mak her a woman,*
> *Tak her below an mak—'*

Judith recoiled in disgust. Only sinners and sea-dogs would be as brazen to utter such vulgarities of the Blessed Mother. She tried covering her ear with her upper arm but it was no use. Even though she'd often heard this shanty from the men back at the castle as they asked what to do with the drunken soldier, never before had she heard such blasphemous verses.

It had even been a favourite of her late husband. He'd sing it to keep the morale of the men raised as they performed menial tasks like tending to the animals or harvesting the crop. He even had a special verse he'd sing to her.

He'd sneak up behind her as she spun the loom, wrap his arms around her waist, and whisper in her ear, 'What shall I do wi me beautiful lady...'

Judith wept at the thought of her husband, adding fresh salt to her bloodied lips. The previous day may have been the first time since losing him she hadn't reminisced. There was so much going on at the castle, she barely had the chance to breathe.

The earl had thrown the most splendid banquet, celebrating the reprieve of his friend, Minister David Dickson. The minister had been stripped of his parish for his vociferous criticism of the Five Articles of Perth. He was permitted to remain at the castle and not have to face the authorities, under the condition he did not set foot inside a church to preach a sermon. Judith suspected he was disappointed not to get his day in court – he did love a debate. Unwearied, dogged, and a captivating speaker, he would have let the high commission know *exactly* what he thought of their religious reforms.

And so, the folk came in their droves from every corner of the parish. Every church must have lain empty yesterday as the crowd at the great gate grew. Weary the mood of the folk might turn sour, the earl permitted the minister to speak. The great hall would not suffice, so they held proceedings in the gardens.

The sun shone brightly and the Minister spoke beautifully, bathing the eager masses in a joy that makes life worth living. His sermon was, as always, varied and enthralling. From his banishment and the dangers of conceding even these small reforms to the papal tyranny, all the way to the validity of the witch trials sweeping the nation. The countess played hymns on the virginals, and all in attendance sang with such vociferous passion, the angels above surely wept tears of joy.

Judith tugged at her bonds and wondered if the angels now wept tears of sorrow for her.

As wonderful as the sermon had been, the best was yet to come. The day was rounded off by the countess's dear friend and guest of honour, Elizabeth Melville. Better known as Lady Culross, she is the first female Scots writer to see her work in print. She arrived at the castle not one week earlier. Judith spent the entire week trying to put herself in Lady Culross's company. However, whenever she managed so, she failed to summon the courage to speak to her, let alone beg to hear her poems. Fortunately, the crowd requested on her behalf yesterday.

Judith sat on the trodden grass in awe at the poet lady's words. It was as if they were the only two there, the only two in the world, as the poet's verses tugged at her heart and prodded her mind.

Judith spoke with her afterwards when most folk had gone home.

Truth be told, it's more accurate to say she stood with her mouth ajar as the remaining guests conversed with the poet lady. Nevertheless, Lady Culross's tenacity and enthusiasm for poetry had inspired her. Judith retired early with quill, ink and parchment in hand, filled with dreams of following the great woman's footsteps and penning verses that one and all would love. Words that might make a difference.

That's when she first encountered *him.*

As is custom, the earl invited the master of any ship at port to his banquets. One such ship was the *NINE*, sailing out of Barra.

A shadow crept over her as she entered her quarters. She turned to be confronted by *him.*

He introduced himself with all the pompous entitlement of a spoiled king. 'Good Lady, allow me to introduce myself. I am Niall MacNeil, nephew of the great MacNeil of Barra, master of the *NINE*, greatest ship in all the Western Isles, therefore, the world. It's a pleasure to make your acquaintance.' He kissed her hand and bowed deeply as if she were a royal highness, all the while keeping his beady eyes fixed on hers.

Although he presented himself as noble – with his plaid proudly displaying his clan colours, buckles and buttons shining, his red-hair restrained under a bonnet, and his pointy little beard groomed – she had heard tales of his kin. His uncle was infamous and better known as Rory the Turbulent. A name well suited to a clan birthed, bred and buried upon the waves.

They had the blood of norsemen and the ancient people of this land pulsing through them. Those heathen ones who practiced ungodly ways so common before Christ saved us all. Although their clan claimed to be Christian, rumours abound they still idolised the pagan gods of old.

The MacNeil's call themselves privateers. Their detractors say sea dogs. Some claim they are spoilers. Others go as far as naming them plundering robbers on the high sea.

The MacNeil's are pirates, so feared and treacherous, Queen Elizabeth had entreated her cousin's son, King James, to bring them to heel. When summoned before the king, Rory the Turbulent managed to save his neck by stating he thought to do his majesty a service by harassing the woman who killed his mother. Very cunning indeed.

Judith had returned pleasantries with Niall MacNeil before excusing herself. It wasn't enough for a man seemingly accustomed to getting what he wanted.

'Good Lady,' he said, placing an arm across the door, 'I beg of you. Do not deny me the name of the most beautiful woman my world-weary eyes have ever had the pleasure to sup on.'

At the time, she considered it *was* rude not to offer her name. Given the chance to relive the moment she would claw those beady eyes from his head.

She apologised and introduced herself while trying to make it clear she would rather be elsewhere. He was either too simple to notice, or too conceited to care. He prattled on about how it would be most pleasing if a fine lady such as herself would honour him and spend the evening aboard his ship, dining with a son of the oldest clan in the world.

When she returned, 'I suppose you MacNeil's were on the ark.'

He smirked and said, 'Nae, we had our own boat.'

Despite the arrogance of the comment it did make her laugh. She smiled, thanked him for the offer, but refused. He smiled and bowed again. Judith took her leave, closed the door to her quarters and locked it – glad to be rid of him.

At the time, she thought her encounter with the MacNeil was not an overly terrible one – it *had* kindled the flame of inspiration. She lit some candles, sat at her dresser, and scribbled the words that would make her famous. The feathered quill flowed across the parchment as if an angel had taken control of her hand. She finished and read over her words... and again...and again. She thought them nowhere near as powerful as the lady poet's, but everyone must start somewhere. Contented, she changed into her favourite deep-blue nightgown, blew out the candles, and got into her comfy bed. Judith fell asleep with her poem running through her mind.

Come ye MacNeil, with your banner, so proud
Come ye MacNeil, with your arrogance, so loud
Your fine cloths and sweet scents, might trick a less-er lass
But not me or my kin, we can see through your brass

Come ye MacNeil, your a pirate, we ken
Come ye MacNeil, you'll get chased down the glen
Your fast boat and cunning, reigns supreme on the sea
But here in the lord's lands, he does watch over me

* * *

Judith's dreams of poetry ended as her waking nightmare began – with a rough hand pressed over her mouth, and a sharp blade held at her throat. Her eyes needed no time to adjust. Sweet perfume and whispered words of, 'Nobody denies a MacNeil,' told her who accosted her.

The journey in the dark – first on manback, then on horseback – had been a rushed, bumpy one, filled with terrible thoughts of slavery, torture, rape and murder. She struggled to breathe with the bag over her head, and the thick rope binding her hands cut into her wrists. Her thighs and nightgown were sodden with the contents of her bladder.

Overwhelming panic ensued when the scent of the sea wafted through the bag. She struggled harder and screamed muffled cries for help, knowing any hope of rescue would soon vanish. A thumping blow to the side of her head was the last thing she remembered before waking on an unfamiliar bed in a dark room.

She regained her senses as panic flooded her. She was bound to a bed, had a gag over her mouth, and the room felt as though it was swaying. She quickly realised the swaying meant she was on a ship. She let out a muffled wail, desperate for someone, *anyone*, to come to her aid.

That's when she sensed *him*.

Her heightened senses caught that sweet perfume.

A match sizzled to life, partly illuminating him. He lit a candle and moved slowly towards her.

She struggled against her bonds and cried out.

He reached her, placed the candle on a holder above the bed, and moved his face close so their noses almost touched. Flames danced in his beady eyes.

She turned her head to the side.

He tore the gag from her mouth with his teeth and whispered, 'Louder, m' lady. I do love it when they scream.' His breath like a thousand spiders crawling over her exposed neck.

A shout from above of 'Ship at sea!' ended any hope she still clung to.

He entered her as his ship entered the ocean.

After, as he pulled his trews up, he called it a quick docking to get acquainted. He removed her gag and told her to call out when her heart could bear their parting no more. He snuffed the candle before leaving her with the words, 'We shall know each other more...*intimately*, before our voyage comes to an end.'

Judith had lain awake in the darkness for what seemed an eternity in despondent numbness interspersed with bouts of extreme terror. While from above, her captors laughed, sang, stomped their feet in time with fiddles, and plotted God knows whatever else.

God knows...

Does he know?

Does he know the pain she is in?

Does he know how cruelly she had been treated?

Does he know how bad this voyage will become?

Does he know how it will end?

Does he even care?

She broke down again. Not only had that *man* captured, beaten and defiled her, he now made her question the good lord.

'Forgive me, Father,' she whispered between sobs. 'I know not what to think. Please, I beg, give me strength. Please, Good Lord, help me in my darkest hour.'

Thoughts of her previous most faith-trying time sprang to mind. She shook her head as if trying to shake off the emotion washing over her.

'Why...why...why...' she sobbed.

The first grey slithers of dawn glowed through the small porthole at the far side of the captain's quarters. The cabin – prison to her – was no bigger than her room back at the castle. Dark stained wood was broken only by a rug in the centre. It was still too dim to discern its colour. To her right was an alcove with a desk strewn with various parchments and what looked to be navigation equipment. The only door lay at the far side of the desk. The small bed she was bound to was also in an alcove and had a mirror running its full length.

The chaffing of rough rope on broken skin drew her attention. She turned onto her back and glanced up at her wrists. Her stomach turned and skin crawled at the well-worn post she was bound to. How many women had experienced the advances of this *man*. More importantly, what had become of them?

Loud belly-laughs from above startled her from desperate thoughts. She held her breath and listened – footsteps descending a staircase.

'No,' she begged. 'Please, God, no.'

The footsteps got louder as her heart beat quicker.

Her whole body trembled.

The footsteps stopped.   Heavy breathing and muttering seeped through the wooden door.

She flinched when the door handle rattled.

She closed her eyes tight and breathed deeply in the vain attempt to compose herself before turning on to her side with her back to the door.

The door creaked open and someone stumbled in, slamming it behind them.

'Ssshhh...comp-company...sleeping...ssshhh...'

It was *him*.

She did her best impression of someone sleeping as his drunken steps approached.

He leant on the edge of the bed and she almost screamed when he kissed her cheek and slithered his tongue in her ear.

'S-so beut-hic-beautiful...' He tugged at her bonds. 'Come on, damn thing...'

The tight bonds on her wrists eased, allowing blood to flow back into her hands. This respite was overshadowed by the terrifying question of where he was taking her. Her bottom lip quivered and a tear sailed down her cheek as the drunken pirates up-top sprang to mind.

'That's be-bet...good...'

The bonds eased completely and for the first time since this hellish voyage began, Judith could move her hands. She feigned sleep while adjusting herself and moved her hands under her head. She let out a contented moan before continuing her deep breathing bordering on snoring.

She felt him sit on the edge of the bed. Judith half opened an eye and peered into the mirror. His wild hair hung free and he was leaning forward, fumbling with something at his feet. He sat up and she closed her eye. Something tumbled and banged across the cabin.

He fumbled again.

Judith opened both eyes and turned her head.

He was leaning forward, removing his other shoe.

Her heart quickened at the sight of something hanging on his belt.

The key...a way out...a dagger.

She grabbed the hilt, yanked the dagger free, drew her hand behind her head, and with all the force she could muster, drove it into her captor's back.

He inhaled sharply and sat erect as his hand scrambled to reach the weapon buried hilt deep in his back.

She sprang up, pushed herself into the corner of the bed, and pulled her legs tight against her chest as her whole body trembled.

His breathing was quick and tortured as he struggled to his feet and turned − a look of shock and horror contorted his face. He coughed and sputtered, sending blood spraying from his mouth as he fumbled for his sword. He gurgled as blood poured from his mouth, turning his beard a different shade of red.

Judith winced and closed her eyes.

He let out a ghastly moan before his tortured breathing ceased.

A thud caused Judith to flinch and let out a yelp.

She stole a peek − he was gone.

She crept forward and peered over the bed. His lifeless body lay slumped on the floor with the dagger protruding from his back − the red stain on his white ghillie-shirt growing. She scrambled away and curled into the foetal position − her teeth rattling as she shook like a tree in a stiff breeze.

Dear God, what had she done? Judith rubbed her arms as a mother would to an inconsolable child. She had *killed* a man. A monsterous one, but still a man, and *she* had murdered him. Tears and snot pooled between her cheek and pillow.

'Dear God,' she whispered, 'please forgive me. I did not want to...I *had* to.'

She shook her head as the last time she saw her husband alive came to mind. He too had uttered those words when she begged him not to go.

He had to answer his earl's call.

He had to do his duty.

He had to protect his land, home and kin against those who would destroy it.

He had to ride into the unknown.

He had to charge down the numerically superior Reivers.

He had to take a bullet.

He had to die.

He had to leave her.

How many had died throughout the ages because a sin *had* to be committed? For a fleeting moment, anger reared its head, but the fear coursing through her was all-encompassing.

She remembered how serene her husband had been that day, how brave he looked, and she asked how he could be without fear. He laughed and said he wasn't. No one is. He had merely learned to use it for the good.

'Fear is like fire,' he told her. 'Respect it, learn to harness it, and it will cook your meals and warm your toes. Disrespect it, allow it to run wild, and it will consume you and all around you. My only fear is setting eyes upon you no more.'

Judith remembered how his brave facade almost slipped before he composed himself.

'A pointless fear,' he continued. 'For if the Good Lord decides my time upon this realm is to end, it would only be a brief parting, for we shall reunite in the Kingdom of Heaven.'

Judith begged him to promise he'd return.

A mischievous smile crossed his lips. 'As long as you promise to have my favourite supper ready when I do.' She feigned anger before he embraced her. 'Good, anger is also a strong emotion you must learn to harness. It can rouse one to action.'

He never did sup with her that evening. Or the next. Nor any since.

Judith sat upright and swung her legs over the side of the bed. Her eyes fell upon the slain pirate and her jaw clenched. She could still feel his seed inside her. She gripped the bed sheets as bile bubbled up inside before spilling out.

'You bastard,' she growled. 'You heartless, godless, evil, son of a filthy whore!' She spat her words in a crescendo.

Her eyes shot to the door. She had no idea what lay beyond, how many men crewed the ship, their location, and if they could hear her. She sprang to her feet, snatched the chair, and wedged it underneath the handle.

Judith scanned the cabin. A chest lay at the foot of the bed. She made for it, keeping her distance from the blood-soaked pirate.

'God damn it,' she cursed at the heavy iron chain securing the chest.

She turned. The desk had drawers below it. Judith made for it, this time stepping over the corpse. She opened the first drawer and smiled at its contents – a large pistol. She snatched the long, sleek, heavy weapon from the drawer. The contrast between warm wood and cold metal comforted her. Never in her life had she held a gun, and she had no idea if it was even loaded. She peered down the hole at the end, almost certain that was where the shot went.

From the same drawer, Judith lifted a small flask and a cloth bag. She untied the bag and found around twenty lead shots wrapped in paper. A slight scent of charcoal wafted from the flask as she uncorked it. She had seen plenty of guns being fired but cursed herself for never paying attention.

She was sure the gunpowder went in first, but unsure of how much. Better too much than too little. She poured a considerable amount into the muzzle with most spilling over the sides onto her hand. Judith dropped a single shot into the muzzle.

Uncertain what to do next, she sighed and shook her head. 'What am I thinking?'

There wasn't a hope in hell that she could simply pop upstairs, point a pistol at an unknown number of pirates – who'd have weapons of their own they knew how to use – and force them to take her home. It's more likely they would shoot to injure so they may torture their captain's murderer.

Judith tossed the pistol on to the desk in disgust. 'How in God's name can I make them turn about?'

She wondered if offering coin would work. If there was one sureness regarding pirates it was their greed motivated them above all else. She sighed and shook her head. The fact they were scoundrels did not equate to them being simpletons. They'd reason as soon as Judith was safely ashore she would scream blue murder and they'd be hunted down.

Her body trembled again as paralysing fear threatened to consume her.

Thoughts of her husband's last conversation came to mind – 'No one is fearless.'

She racked her brain, trying to figure out what pirates fear. Every man, woman and child is not without fear. Their own personal unknown they cannot step into. But what keeps pirates awake at night? As a group they are among the most fearless there are, but under their gruff exterior, they are flesh, blood, and bone like the rest. They are mere men.

'That's it!'

Men fear what they do not know, and what they truly can never know are women.

Tales of the most fearsome woman she had ever heard of came to mind, and a plan came together in a torrent. One so ludicrous and outlandish, it may actually work. Four years previously, a local woman by the name of Margaret Barclay had struck fear into every man, woman and child in her parish. A big shouldered borough that does not normally frighten easily.

Tiny hairs on her arms stood on end as she removed her nightgown. Her eyes fell upon the pooling blood on the pirate's back. Judith knelt beside him, glanced towards the heavens, and offered a silent prayer.

She tore the blood-drenched shirt open, inhaled deeply, and dipped her hands into the warm pool of blood. She retched, withdrew her blood-stained hands, and used them to scribe over her arms, legs and torso. Judith drew symbols of serpents, spirals and reverse crosses. She made random markings one might consider an archaic language. She worked the blood through her hair, making it stand on end. She stood facing the mirror and drew a five-star pendant upon her chest before smearing the remainder around her mouth.

The sun had yet to rise but enough light bathed the cabin for her to behold her work. She looked ghastly, a true representation of evil, but was it enough? Judith shuddered as an idea popped to mind.

She squatted by the pirate's corpse and pulled the dagger from his back with a squelch. The lifeless pirate was a heavy lump, but she managed to roll him onto his back. She tilted his head back, withdrew his sword from its scabbard, and stood. The longsword was so heavy, she had to hold it with both hands.

Judith glanced towards the heavens. 'Forgive me, Father.'

She inhaled deeply, raised the sword high above her head, and with all her might, swung it down upon Niall's exposed neck. Blood splattered, making a horrible squelch along with a thud as the end of the sword struck the wooden cabin floor. Her eyes darted to the door and she froze. Satisfied no one had heard, she turned to examine her blow.

Judith winced and fought the urge to vomit at Niall MacNeil's head barely clinging to his body. She stepped back before delivering the next cut – this time dropping to one knee to lessen the arc. An unsettling triumph swept over Judith as Niall's head became liberated from his body.

She grabbed the head by the hair – it was heavier than a basket full of potatoes. She crept to the door, sat the sword against the desk, removed the chair, and opened the door.

She peeked out – the coast was clear.

With sword in one hand, head in the other, and every butterfly on God's earth seemingly fluttering in her tummy, Judith ascended the stairs to begin her bid for freedom.

She reached the top deck and paused. Silence shrouded the ship and a blood-red sky hung over the land to the east. A chilly breeze buffeted her, causing the goose-bumps covering her naked body to worsen. A single man sat at the helm with his back to her. This would be more believable if done before sunrise.

Judith took a lung full of sea air, pulled her chin close to her chest, narrowed her eyes, bared her teeth, and growled.

The helmsman glanced over his shoulder, double-taking before jolting to his feet. He looked barely old enough to marry. The boy's mouth hung open, his lower jaw trembling as he backed away before thumping against the wheel.

Judith continued snarling as she took slow, deliberate, thudding steps towards him.

He glanced over his shoulder as if looking for help. He seemed close to either screaming, fleeing, or wetting himself.

'Your crew,' Judith growled, pointing the sword at him. 'Beckon them.'

His lips moved but no words came out. All colour drained from his face and his eyes darted between Judith and the severed head of his captain.

'THE BELL!' she roared.

He startled to action, almost tripping as he darted for the ship's bell.

He rang it like a man possessed.

Good. The crew will be on edge before they even set eyes upon her.

Judith glanced around – her eyes resting on the ship's anchor. Perfect. She went to it and knelt, laying the head and sword before her. She pushed two fingers past the layer of congealed blood along Niall's neck – it was no longer warm. She smeared markings onto the anchor before pushing the sword deep inside the head. She placed both hands on top of the anchor and chanted unintelligible words.

The ship came alive with hurried footsteps and banging doors. Mumbled questions were being asked. Still, the bell tolled.

'Ciaran!' someone called. 'Rest that bloody bell.'

The bell fell silent. Judith continued chanting.

'Wit in God's name is the meaning o' this?'

'It's...it's...'

'Wit is it?'

Judith swayed and chanted louder.

'It's...'

'Spit it oot, boy!'

'It's a bastard witch!'

She sprang to her feet, turned, and held the sword with the severed head atop before her. She growled, snarled, and lunged for the crew, thrusting their captain's head towards them.

They were half-dressed, bleary-eyed, and visibly shocked. They froze for a moment before pulling an array of weapons. Around two dozen men pointed swords, daggers and pistols in her direction. One even ran and hid behind a barrel. Pirates are superstitious, but were they falling for it?

'Kill her!' one of them yelled.

Apparently, not yet. Judith kept in character, showing no fear, even though inside she was flapping like a moth on a spider web. The standoff was tense. The crew glanced at one another, asking silent questions.

No answers were given.

'I said kill her,' the same man said, the confidence fading from his command.

'Kill her yerself,' offered another.

Judith flung her head back and laughed hysterically. She lowered her gaze and snarled at the stunned crew.

'If none among you,' she said, slow and deliberate, 'are man enough to make a decision. Perhaps you should seek guidance from your captain.'

Confused faces glanced at one another.

Judith grabbed their captain's head by the hair and pulled it from his sword with a squelch. She wedged the point of the sword between the planks of the deck. The crewmen had formed a semi-circle around her. She stepped forward, holding the severed head before her. They all shuffled away.

'Anyone?' she snarled, moving the head from side to side. 'No?' She shook her head. 'Tut-tut-tut. Lost lambs without their shepherd's guidance. I shall converse with him on your behalf.'

Judith held Niall's head up to hers with his mouth next to her ear. She kept it there while she nodded and periodically giggled.

The crew leaned in as if trying to hear.

'I shall inform them, *Captain*.'

Judith thrust the head before her.

'I riled a demon, a witch o' the night
Me soul now screams ghastly, in terrible fright
If ye no wish tae join me, in the fires o' hell
Ye'll turn this ship aboot, lest ye sink in the swell
These dark hands that slither, upon me cold lifeless head
Cursed me weapon in hand, in me own cosy bed
Its black heart has sworn, those who kill it in spite

Will join me forever, in the cold endless night
If by nightfall this beast, still sails, on the sea
Then the anchor it's cursed, will drown, all of thee.'

Judith turned Niall's head to face her and held it with both hands. 'Beautiful! My *Captain*.' She cackled before planting her lips upon the captain's. She slurped her tongue in and out of his mouth while keeping her eyes locked on the one who called to kill her.

Horrified gasps bounded around the crew. One man vomited where he stood, too frozen with fear to move to the side of the ship.

'She's in league wae the devil.'

'Show us mercy.'

'Jesus, help us.'

The sneering smile Judith felt cross her lips was genuine. She had fooled them.

'Nae, I still say we kill it. It's the only way tae break the curse.' A few dissenting voices joined the man showing resistance. He was beginning to tick her off. 'And wit's tae stop it betraying us once we're ashore?'

'Kill I, and you die,' Judith said. 'Betray you, and we *all* die. For in my land, only witches are feared and despised above pirates.' She cackled as the thought of Margaret Barclay crossed her mind. 'Yet one option remains, my salty spoilers. Trust. Trust between the two most untrustworthy kinds. Witches and pirates.'

That silenced the doubters. The crew looked at one another, seemingly waiting for one of their number to make the call.

What else could be done to convince them?

The sun poked above the hills to the east. Judith screamed and dropped Nial's head, startling many of the pirates. She grabbed the sword, growled, hissed, and jabbed the sword at the sun as she skulked away. She descended the stairs, let out a blood-curdling cackle, and slammed the door to the captain's cabin behind her. She dropped the sword and pressed her ear against the timber door.

No one spoke for what seemed an eternity before bickering erupted. The one who called for her death did most of the talking.

'I've seen it done,' he said. 'Ye strangle em an burn em.'

'At the same time?'

'Aye, I think so.'

'How in God's name dae ye dae that withoot torchin yersel?'

'Ye use a rope! Ya buffoon.'

'And just how dae we burn a witch withoot settin the ship ablaze? Ya *bloody* buffoon.'

'Ahh, christ, I've been cursed tae sail wae a bunch o' simpletons an cowards. We tak it ashore.'

'Wit aboot the curse?'

There was a pause and Judith held her breath. Was he waning?

'I'm sure,' said her nemesis, 'killing it that way, *should* break the curse.'

'Should? Is that the best ye can offer?'

'I'm no a bloody priest!'

'Naw, yer no, yer a half-wit at best.'

The crew erupted into discernable bickering.

'RIGHT!' roared a voice she hadn't yet heard. 'Wheesht! The lot o' ye's. The only way tae settle this wae nae captain and nae time tae pick a new yin, is by vote. Raise yer hawn, if ye agree wae Dougal. We tak it ashore an kill it.'

There was a moment's pause before he continued. 'Raise yer hawn, if ye agree wae...the captain, an we tak her hame.'

Judith prayed the majority had voted for this.

'An joost keep yer hawns doon if yer no man enough tae make a decision. Bloody cowards. So be it.'

Thumping and banging came from above as the men got to work. The ship lurched as it changed direction.

Judith slumped against the door, took a deep, shuddering breath, and slid down to the cabin floor.

She had played her hand – given it her best. All she could do now was wonder. Wonder what their decision was. Wonder which direction they sailed. Wonder where she would spend the night. Home or hell.

NEVER KID A KIDDER

'Happy April Fools, ya bloody eejits,' I say as I set the last orange traffic-cone down.

I close the zipper on my shopping trolley and toddle homeward. Apart from the wakening birds, my street's quieter than a deaf-mute's parrot at this time on a Sunday morning. If only they toerag's up the stairs were the same. Barely slept a wink last night, what with the music and the like. If ye can even call it that. All boom boom boom and electronic tunes made on a computer. Do bands even play instruments these days?

I chuckle at myself – these days. I've still enough marbles left to remember rolling my eyes and sighing when my wee granny said that to me.

'You young-yins don't know what music is,' she'd tell me. 'Louis Armstrong and The Andrews Sisters, now there's good music. Not like your Beatles and Monkees. And why do they all call themselves after animals? Is the name their parents gave them no good enough? And don't even get me *started* on their haircuts.'

Now *I'm* the granny and here I am, parroting her. I wonder how much of an old fuddy-duddy my own grandweans think of me. I don't think Charles does. Not after our last Christmas day out, anyway. He was my first grandchild and will always hold a special place in my heart. He's almost a man now, and I know there's a million and one things he'd rather be doing than traipsing around the Christmas market with his gran, but it's so hard to let them go. He'll understand when he's a grandparent himself. Not that I'll be around to see that...

Anyway, I'm sure he's gained a new-found respect for me after our wee day out last Christmas. The rest will likely still see me as a boring old woman. Christopher, Isla, Oliver, Lilly, Curtis, and Rebecca are still too young, but it'll come. I wonder what they'll think of their own grandweans taste in music. That's the *real* circle of life.

Mr Singh opens his shop's shutters, shattering the early morning peace. He's reliable as old boots. Every morning for as long as I can remember, come hell or high water, he's there, opening up for this community. Sure, his stuff might not be as cheap as they fancy supermarkets. And yes, some of his stock is well-past its best, but at least ye get a friendly face and a good old chin-wag. Some of the workers in they supermarkets are staler than Mr Singh's loafs. You know, the ones barely able to conceal their contempt, and it's clear they'd much rather be elsewhere. I grudge giving them my money. I've never known the Singh's to take a day off, never mind a holiday, and there's more than a few people on this estate that owe them a lot. The Singh's are good folk. The types who wouldnae see anyone short of a loaf or pint of milk if they were struggling.

'Happy April Fools, Jasmeet.'

He jumps and spins around – his eyes as wide as the Clyde. 'Jesus, Jean, I nearly jumped oot ma turban. Are you trying tae bury me?'

I laugh. 'Aye, Karminder's promised halfers on yer life insurance if I bump ye off.'

'My only goal left in life is tae make sure I outlive that sour-faced bastardin wife of mine, so you'll need tae try harder than that.'

'Challenge accepted.'

He smiles through his scraggly grey beard. 'You're early this mornin.'

'I am so. All the family's coming round today. I had...something to do before they arrive.'

'Aw, good stuff, Jean,' he says as he shuffles through his keys. 'Wit's the occasion? It's no your birthday, is it?'

'No, no,' I say, shaking my head. 'You know, when women get to a certain age we stop celebrating birthdays.'

'Aye, that bastard of mine must've stopped when she was about five. No because she didnae want to face up to the truth, more because she's a miserable cow.'

I laugh. 'I'll tell her that, so I will.'

He slips a key into the door lock. 'I hope ye do. Gettin a rise out of her is the only joy I've got left.'

'Aye, Karminder's told me all about how she loves "getting a rise" out of you.'

He pauses and turns to me, barely able to contain his smirk. 'Any more of that talk and I'll be scrubbin your mouth out wae soap.' He puts an ancient, bony shoulder into the door and opens it. 'So, if it's no yer birthday, what's the occasion?'

'It's...' I glance away and nibble my lip, '...an anniversary. Ten years the day ma Terrance died.'

He glances skyward and sighs. 'Shit, Jean, of course – April Fools Day. I'm sorry, I should've remembered. Come away in.' He switches the lights on and holds the door open. 'There's a seat behind the till. Plunk yerself down and I'll away through the back and make us a brew.'

'Thanks, but I'm wanting back up the road sharp. You know, to get the housework done before the clan gets here.'

'Are ye sure?'

'Positive. Plus, I'm hoping to get a cheeky wee hour on the couch. Barely slept a wink last night with they noisy buggers up the stairs.'

'Were they arseholes partying again?'

Partying? More like raving and driving *me* raving mad. 'Well, it is the weekend.'

He shakes his head and scowls. 'They're wanting a boot in the baws, that lot. Do you know they had the cheek tae ask for tick for their carry-out yesterday? If I'd known they would be keeping you up I would've chased them.'

'Och, don't be daft, they'd just get it somewhere else after giving you a mouthful. It's really no that bad. It's only really the weekends they party now.'

'Every weekend?' He says, raising his brow.

Without fail. 'Sometimes, but don't you be getting yerself into trouble on my account.'

'I'll be telling them wit's wit next time I see them.'

Typical Mr Singh – very low tolerance for idiots. A need for running a business round here. 'You be careful. You're no a young man anymore.'

'Jean, I was never a young man. As soon as they could, ma bastard parents married me off to that morale hoover.'

I laugh. If you think Mr Singh dishes it out about his wife, you should hear what she says about him. But you know, I've yet to see them bicker, never mind show any *real* hostility towards each other.

'Anyway,' he says, 'sit yerself down and I'll get yer shoppin.' He picks up a basket. 'So, that's ten years Terry's been gone?'

'It is so,' I say as I sit on the comfy chair behind the till. 'That's why all the family's coming round today. You know, they've never said so, but I suspect they don't want me being alone on this day.'

'It's a good bunch you've got there. You must be proud.'

'I am so.'

He shakes his head slightly as his eyes drift skyward. 'I can't believe Terry's been gone that long.' I know. I still have to pinch myself too. 'Feels like only yesterday he was coming in for his papers and rolls.' What about his lager and fags? 'Terry was a diamond, and I've yet tae hear a bad word spoke about him.' Oh, I could give ye a whole book full of bad words about him. 'It's never the ones ye want that go early.' He shakes his head. 'So, wit ye after, Jean?'

'Right, I'm needin three pints of milk. One red one for Kirsten, a pint of the green for Stephen, Murray, wee Chloe and Knox, and everyone else is fine with the blue. You know what, better make it two pints of the blue.'

He goes to the fridge and shouts, 'Got them. Wit else?'

'I'll need four loafs. Two white, one brown for Stephen, Kirsten, Ben, wee Calvin and Charlie, and James and wee James like the plain bread.'

He goes to the bread aisle. 'Good gear or cheap shite?'

I laugh. 'Only the best for my family.'

'Goes without saying. Right, are ye needin any fish tae feed yer five thousand?'

'No, no, Jasmeet, but I do need a couple packs of chopped pork. Charles, wee Joe, and my Stephen love that. I'll take a jar of chicken paste for Harris, Roamin, Lilly, and Cairn. A jar of salmon paste for Ashton, Oliver, Chloe, Curtis, and Charlie. A packet of chicken roll for Christopher and Jack, and a couple packets of roast ham for everybody else.'

'Anything else?'

'Just some biscuits.'

Mr Singh heads to the biscuit section. 'Wit kind?'

'Have ye any of they big boxes of Mcvities Family Circle?'

'Of course I do.'

'Are they in date?'

'Cheeky bugger.' He pops his head above the shelves – a fake look of offence on his grizzled face. 'Any more of that and you'll be getting barred for life.'

I laugh. 'Best grab some Angel Slices as well if ye have any. I don't like giving the younger ones biscuits in case they choke. Oh, and a packet of Yum-Yums as well. Charles loves them.'

Mr Singh sets the overflowing basket on the counter before joining me behind the till and ringing up my stuff.

'So,' he says, 'what's the plan? A spot of lunch and a blether?'

I nod and smile. 'If the weather holds we'll maybe take a wee walk down to the river and feed the ducks with any leftover bread.'

He lifts his head and looks at me. 'Do you still remember how tae use the till?'

'Of course I do. It's like riding a bike.'

'Here then. You finish ringing this up, I'll be back in a jiffy.'

Mr Singh disappears through the back. I stand and finish ringing up and bagging my shop. As I'm fetching my purse from my handbag, Mr Singh appears with four loafs.

'Here ye are, Jean. Like the apple-of-my-eye still lying in her pit upstairs, these are well-past their best. Take them for the grandweans tae feed the ducks.'

'Och, that's good of you, Jasmeet.' I hand him the money. 'You know, they ducks will struggle keepin afloat after all this.'

He laughs and grabs the bags, puts them into my shopping trolley. 'Don't mention it. Always a pleasure, never a chore.' He holds the door open. 'And remember, if any of your brood are wanting sweeties, be sure tae send them here.'

I toddle out. 'Will do, Jasmeet. I'll see ye later and thanks a lot.'

'See ye after, Jean.'

I'm at my house in no time at all. Looks like them up the stairs have called it a night – the music's stopped and curtains drawn. Bloody vampires. Although to be fair, vampires are less life-draining than these fruit-bats.

I leave my shopping trolley at the front door and head round the back with one of the stale loafs Mr Singh gave me. Just as suspected – they idiots up the stairs have no bothered taking in the washin they hung out yesterday afternoon.

I open the loaf and throw the lot into their garden.

'Happy April Fools, ya noisy bastards.'

Before I've even got the gate closed the first of the bombers lands to load up. I smile and head in the house.

After making the sandwiches, I cleaned the kitchen and toilet, mopped the floors, and hoovered. Just a quick dust-down and polish, and I'll maybe have time for forty winks.

I polish the ornaments at the foot of the fireplace, and put them on the mantelpiece out of reach of tiny fingers. I pick up the silver-framed wedding photo of me and Terrance, give it a skoosh of furniture polish, and wipe it with a duster.

What a day that was. Everyone there said so. You know, even today when reminiscing about the good auld days with anyone left alive who was at my wedding, they all have fond memories of that day. I hold the picture up and strain my eyes. I look so beautiful. And happy. I remember thinking this was just the beginning of the fairy tale. Little did I know it would be less Hans Christian Anderson, and more The Brothers Grimm.

It was fitting Terrance went on April Fools Day as he was a bit of a joker himself. Always winding up and playing practical jokes on his workmates or pals down the pub.

Like the time he got them all with the joke lighter he'd bought in Blackpool. You know, the one that delivers an electric shock when ye press the button.

Comedy gold.

Or the time he convinced them a junkie had mugged him after lifting his wages from the bank. He drank for free that night and walked away with over six hundred pounds in his pocket. Three hundred from the whip-round they had to replace his stolen wages, and the three hundred that had supposedly been stolen. The young team went on a 'junkie hunting' spree that lasted months after they found out what 'happened' to Terrance.

An absolute barrel of laughs.

It wasn't just his pals or work mates that bore the brunt of his jokes. I did too. Like how he always joked that as the years went on, my boobs got saggier while my touch got firmer.

The funny bugger.

Or when he'd had a drink or twelve, he'd always joke that he ended up with the wrong sister.

Classic Terrance.

Ye see, him and his pal Frank, chatted me and my sister up while we waited on a bus after the dancing. Frank winched Cathie for a few weeks, but that's as far as their fling went. I ended up marrying Terrance.

I think the biggest trick he ever pulled on me was making me feel sorry for him after he'd let his fists fly when he was drunk. The funny bugger even made me think *I* was to blame.

After all, it's not a wife's place to answer her husband back, is it?

As the years dragged by, that trick became less and less funny. But you know, I was in on the joke, so felt trapped and unable to tell anyone, not even Cathie. Then nature played the ultimate prank on him.

We were at a wedding reception ten years ago, and he became unwell. His lips swole up slightly. No one noticed, but I did, and he felt it. You know, I did have a wee chuckle inside at Terrance the joker finally getting a bit of comeuppance.

He'd been eating nuts from the bowl at our table all night. Now, up until that point he'd never had an allergic reaction to anything before. I suggested we get him to the hospital, but he was having none of it. We went home, but his condition only got worse. His lips got fatter so that he looked like the young lassies of today with their trout-pout. His tongue matched his lips, so much so, he struggled breathing. You know, he wouldnae even let me call the doctor, the bloody fool. I went to my pals down the road, and she gave me some Piriton she kept in the cupboard as her weans were allergic to everything. I gave him a teaspoon of it and in no time at all, his lips and tongue had returned to their normal size.

He never had another reaction to nuts again...until one week later.

After another of his funny, rib-tickling moments – one I'm sure cracked rather than tickled a rib or two of mine – I made his dinner.

Could barely stand, what with the searing pain in my side, but I managed to cook up a tasty chicken korma for him. He always liked a curry after a hard day spent propping up the bar at his local. I cooked it in a nut oil, and as I could barely read the cook-book with my watery eyes, I couldnae see how much ground up almonds and cashews the recipe called for. So, I dumped the whole lot in.

Better too much than no enough, right?

From the corner of my eye, I watched him finish every last piece.

Before he'd even set his fork down and ordered me to wash his plate, his whole head swole up like a balloon.

Now *he* was the one wanting to call an ambulance.

I was havin none of it.

He collapsed onto the floor, struggling for a breath and unable to speak, but his eyes begged for help.

I flung his mobile phone at him.

His swollen fingers fumbled to unlock it.

Not that he'd have had any joy with normal sized fingers. I wished him a happy April Fools Day, and went for a walk round the block, clutching his phone battery in my pocket.

And so the family come over every April Fools. They don't want me feeling sad on the anniversary of my funny, beloved, nut-intolerant bastard of a husband's death.

The sound of the front door opening followed by tiny feet running up the hall pulls me from memory lane. I set the picture down and turn.

Lilly, Oliver, and Curtis charge into my living room, shouting, 'Granny, Granny,' with their arms open wide and big smiles on their wee cute faces.

I drop to ma knees as quick as these auld legs will allow. The three slam into me, almost knocking me over, and plant kisses on my face and hug me tight.

'My, my,' I say, ruffling their hair and pinching their cheeks. 'Look how big yous are getting!'

'Big and bad,' my Suzanne says, walking into the living room. 'Yous be careful with yer granny.'

'They're fine,' I say, letting them go and struggling to my feet.

'How are ye, Mum?' Suzanne says, helping me up.

'I'm good, hen,' I say as she gives me a hug and a kiss. 'How are you? And where's Charles?'

'He's still in bed.'

'Oh.'

'Don't worry, Mum, he'll be down in a bit.'

'Will he? That's good. Is he still seeing Natalie?'

She nods and raises her brow. 'That's why he's still in bed. First time we've let her stay over last night.'

'Ah, I see.'

'And plus,' my Stephen's wife Kirsten says as she walks into the living room. 'He's hiding from me.' She comes over and gives me a hug and a kiss. 'Stephen'll be here around lunchtime.'

'I know, hen,' I say. 'He texted me to say he'd be late as he was on the night shift last night. Where's Rebecca?'

She pats down her pockets and glances round about herself. 'Shit, Jean, I knew I'd forgot somethin.'

I laugh.

'I've left her sleeping in her pram in the hall. And I'd like it to stay that way for as long as possible, Jean.'

I smile. 'I'm not promising anything but I'll try and no accidentally bump the pram.'

She smiles and shakes her head.

'So,' I say, 'why's Charles hiding from you? What's he done this time?'

She glances at Suzanne and they both share a smirk.

'I'll show ye,' Kirsten says. She turns her attention to the three bairns playing on the floor with each other. 'Curtis, sweetie, come here a wee minute.' Curtis toddles over to his mum. 'Tell granny what big cousin Charles taught you to say.'

Curtis turns to me with the cutest, toothless grin on his cheeky wee face. 'My mummy loves Dickens Cider.'

'She does so, darling,' my Suzanne says with a big smile.

I near choke with laughter. 'What did he say?'

'Dickens, Cider,' Kirsten says, slowly and pronouncing each word properly. 'Wait till I get ahold of that boy.'

'What's he like?' I say. 'Oh, that's the best April fools ever. Right, let me get the kettle on before the rest of the clan arriv—'

'I'll get it, Jean,' Kirsten says, turning for the door.

'Oh, that's good of you, hen.'

'And don't be sneaking into the hall while my backs turned,' she calls.

I smile and sit on the couch. Suzanne joins me.

'Sorry I never had the kettle boiled, but I wasn't expecting yous so early. I've made the sandwiches and got plenty of cakes and biscuits, though.'

'As long as there's none of your *special* brownies,' she says, making air quotes at the word special.

I smile.

'And don't be daft, Mum,' she continues. 'We decided to head over sharp as your street's forever closed off to traffic.'

'Is it?'

She cocks her head slightly and gives me a piercing look. 'Funny thing is, I've yet to see any works being done.'

'Strange thing, that,' I say, trying to sound casual. 'At least the weans can play out the front without us worrying about lunatic drivers flying up and down the road. Oh! That reminds me.' I reach up to the alcove and grab the bag sitting there. 'Come and see what granny's got for yous.'

The three rush over – their faces filled with expectation.

I reach into the bag. 'This is what your granda took to fitba games when he was a wee boy.' I pull one out and give it a whirl. 'Clackers!'

Their wee faces light up as I give them one each.

'Away out the front garden and make as much noise as you want.'

'Your neighbours will love that,' Suzanne says.

I'm particularly hoping the buggers up the stairs will. 'Och, don't worry about them.'

The three weans take off down the hall, shouting, laughing, and making a racket with their new toys. The front door slams followed by a baby's cry.

'JEAN!' Kirsten shouts from the kitchen.

'Oh well,' I say, pushing myself up from the couch. 'I guess I'd better go and see to Rebecca.'

A PLUMS RATING

This! This right here. These muddy boot prints are the perfect example as to why Britain's military is a shadow of its former self. I know *exactly* where they'll lead me. I also know the cretinous slackers who made them should know better. They're a disgrace and an embarrassment, and quite frankly, do not deserve this coveted green beret. I certainly won't miss them and hit the wall.

I turn into the hallway, and as sure as allied ground-troops take cover when USAF planes fly overhead, the shameful trail leads to the mess hall. Barely returned from exercise and already they have the place dirtier than a Bombay brothel. I straighten my beret, dust down my shirt, and march towards the mess.

Muffled chittering becomes clearer as I approach the slightly ajar door. Fucking oafs. Don't they know loose lips sink ships?

I take a deep breath, pat my moustache down, and reach for the door. The mention of my name causes me to pause and cock an ear towards the door.

'...not seen him. Thank fuck.'

'No seen who?'

'You took your time.'

'Aye, I just dropped a thing like King-Kong's thumb in there.'

'One minute longer in the heads and your beer was getting sunk.'

'That's a slashable offence where I come from.'

'*Everything's* a slashable offence where you come from!'

'A bit racist, but I'll let it slide. Who were yous talkin about?'

'Bastard *Cock*burn.'

'Ahh, the clap. Was surprised no to see that crawling cunt stood at the gates, ready to give us an inspection when we got back. And be careful. It's *Sergeant* Cockburn now. Allegedly.'

'Yeah, mate. Promoting snakes like him is precisely why our forces are cattled.'

'Cattled?'

'Yeah, mate – cattle-trucked.'

'Fucked?'

'Clever boy. And here's me thinking you sweaty-sock's all had porridge for brains.'

'Get it up ye, ya Cockney cunt.'

'Listen, when half the good sergeants get medically discharged in Afghanistan and Iraq, and the other half leave for the cash lure of close protection, the only option left is to scrape the barrel. How else do you think cunts like him get promoted after what? Nearly thirty fucking years?'

Cunts like me? Scrape the barrel? Me does detect a hint of jealousy.

'Spot on, mate. Plus the fact our new captain would rather have a dirty Judas in his pocket than a real commando.'

'The pair of them are so low, they should be speaking with an Aussie twang.'

The rest laugh as my fists clench – threaders doesn't even *begin* to describe me.

'They're so brain-dead, they could walk through a horde of zombies, and they wouldn't bat an eyelid.'

'Aye, the kinda cunts who wash paper plates.'

My blood fizzles like I've just been injected with napalm as the laughter intensifies.

'Never thought I'd say this, but the sooner we check into the Basra Hilton the better.'

'What if he comes this time?'

'Are you fuckin jokin? With the amount of salt-water-activated injuries that cunt gets he should be called lifejacket.'

'Fingers crossed the sniveling arse-licker isn't on duty tonight. The lads'll be wanting to let their hair down after those two weeks of hell.'

'And rightly so. I'm tempted to sink a few and join th—'

Bingo. This is precisely the kind of ammunition to knock these insolent bastards down a peg or two.

I wait until the topic of conversation changes before entering the mess. Half a dozen of the worst corporals the Royal Marines have ever known slouch on seats, slugging bottles of beer, watching Match of the Day, and still dressed in their fatigues. Idle bastards. Still wet behind the ear and already promoted to a rank it took me half my bloody career to reach. No wonder the Marines are going to pot.

One turns to me and says, 'G'day, Sergeant.' The rest snigger.

I clear my throat. 'No need to get up, lads.'

'Thanks, Sergeant,' another says. 'We're like fucking *zombies* after that exercise.'

The rest giggle like school girls as my jaw clenches. 'Did you lose your shoe polish and razor blades in the field?'

'There's more important things when on exercise in the Brecon Beacons than shiny shoes,' Corporal Cunninghame says. 'Like keeping your rifle clean. Maybe if you managed along more often you'd realise that.' He doesn't even have the balls to peel his eyes from the television and look me in the eye.

The rest of the corporals do. Like when an out-of-towner walks into a saloon in an old western, the atmosphere pivots to one of tense expectancy. They'll likely be hoping I blow my top. Well, this isn't an episode of *Eastenders*.

I bite my tongue. I won't be baited by this irn-bru-guzzler who's greener than the beret he shamefully wears. 'There are far more important things for someone like me to be doing. I've paid my dues. I was roughing it in the field when you were still a twinkle in your fathers eye.'

Corporal Cunninghame lifts his feet from the chair and spins around to face me. His lips are tighter than the drawstrings to his purse, and his brow's furrowed. 'Wit did you say aboot ma da?' He says, his barbaric twang intensifying with his obvious offence.

Typical fucking Jock – a shorter fuse than an IED. Most of them are nowhere near as deadly, though. All bark and no bite. A whole fucking country suffering from little man syndrome. I fight the urge to push his buttons further. Even though it would be very easy to tip this sweaty-sock over the edge, I don't fancy being on the wrong end of this particular haggis-muncher's wrath. There's a real nastiness to this caber-tosser bubbling below the surface.

The other corporals watch us intently.

I moisten my dry lips. 'May I remind you, *Corporal* Cunninghame, *I* am *your* superior. Be careful with your tone.'

The legal-tender-guru opens his mouth, but Corporal Williamson speaks over the top of him. 'Chill, chill, we're all on the same team here. Sergeant *Cock*burn, what did we miss while we were away?'

Bastard. 'You bloody well know it's pronounced *Coe*-burn.'

Corporal Williamson puts his hands up. 'Apologies, Sergeant *Coe*-burn. So, did much happen around here?'

'I don't suppose any of you lot have bothered doing the rounds yet?' I say.

Corporal Cunninghame turns back to the television and says, 'Aye, *boss*. They're done.'

'When?'

'Earlier, *boss*.'

171

'Define earlier.'

'It means before now,' he says before taking a slug of his beer. 'And here's me thinking you were an educated man...*boss.*'

Smarmy, shortbread-loving git. 'I'm well aware of what it means.'

'Then why did ye ask?'

'I want to know *exactly* when it was done.'

'Ah, that makes sense.'

The others snigger as a wave of heat rushes over my head making me harry redders. 'Corporal Cunninghame, how would you like to be put on charge?'

'No very much, *boss*,' he says.

This deep-fried-connoisseur has a real problem with authority. No doubt he'll be of the ilk that would trade their green beret for an SBS patch in an instant.

'Then tell me *exactly* when you did the rounds,' I demand.

'No can do, *boss*.'

'And why the bloody hell not?'

'Because I don't remember. But, as I'm sure you know, *boss*, it'll be in the logbook.'

'Right,' I seethe. 'I'll be double checking, and if I find one thing out of place – one door unlocked or one drunk bootneck – you can bet Captain Hickinbottom will hear of it first thing in the morning.'

'Come on now, Sergeant,' Corporal Williamson says. 'The lads are cream-crackered. They've sweated their balls off the last two weeks, yomping, eating cold beans, and sharing digs with sheep and cows. Give them a break.'

'Oh, I'm well aware of their sweaty balls. Last time they returned from exercise I caught a bunch of them getting blowjobs from the local trollops through the perimeter fence at the rear of the camp.'

They all laugh at this despicable act.

'Have a heart, Sergeant. By the end of the month they'll be sunning it up on the Costa del Basra.'

'Aye, *boss*,' says Corporal Cunninghame. 'Cut them some slack. They were like *zombies* when they got back. Let them unwind.'

The fucking needle-dropping, trainer-stealing, ginger-haired bastard.

'Right,' I say as I turn and make for the door. 'Mark my words – if I do find them up to no good, they will most certainly be like zombies after the amount of running I'll have them doing.'

I glance over my shoulder as I'm closing the door. Corporal Cunninghame pulls a mobile phone from his pocket. One of those fancy new flip ones, the flash git. No need to even check the logbook – this tells me my suspicions are correct. I make course for the marine's grotts – double marching before Scrooge McWanker can warn them – already picturing the bollocking this lot will get from Captain Hickenbottom.

These corporals – and I use the term loosely – have no idea what makes a good marine. I know they berate me for being a 'model camp commando', but that's a compliment. Much like building a house, strong foundations are required. And I finally have the pleasure of serving a boss who understands this.

I was almost finished with trying to get promoted – almost finished with the military completely – when our new captain told me he needed me for this role. He understands what the service needs is fewer unkempt, undisciplined rogues of the ilk sitting in the mess, and more men like me who respect and love this famed green-lid. Honourable men cut from the cloth of the Duke of York and Albany's Maritime Regiment of Foot. Contrary to what the useless corporals say, *that's* why I've finally been promoted to sergeant. These ruffians have no idea when it comes to the intricacies of serving in Her Majesty's armed forces. You wouldn't believe some of the things they've gotten up to at this camp over the years. Makes me ashamed to be associated with their ilk.

It was around the time when John Major was sorely let down by his party, and had to hand number ten's keys over to Tony Blair and his comrades. Quite frankly, most problems in this country today can be traced to then. I was a newly promoted lance corporal after many unsuccessful – and unjust – attempts. Proud as punch and ready to do Her Majesty's bidding anywhere on land or sea. Perhaps my keenness was why they sent me here – four-five Commando, slap bang in the arsehole of the world.

The missus wasn't best pleased as our daughter had just begun school. I'm obviously inferring as she would never have the gall to question *my* decisions. Not like women today. Always braying about sexism and misogyny and equal rights. I've said it before and I'll say it again – the beginning of the end of our great culture was set in motion the very moment a man's god given right to persuade his spouse with the back of his hand or buckle of his belt was stolen. Mark my words – they'll be allowed to serve on the front lines soon enough. Let's see how many of them take up *that* offer of equality. Thankfully, my beloved corps will never go the way of golf clubs – no woman could ever pass the selection test. Assuming, of course, the goalposts don't get shifted.

My biggest regret about spending almost three fucking socialist parliaments here, is hearing my daughter grow up with that barbaric accent. Everytime she utters the word 'aye' instead of 'yes', or says 'ah ken' instead of 'I know', it's like a bayonet piercing my heart. And believe me, no amount of boarding schools or coercion from myself could prevent it. She's old enough to drive now. Has been for over a year. In a last ditch attempt at saving her decorum, I've told her the only way she'll get lessons and a car from me is if she attends a finishing school for girls. If the stick is out-of-bounds then the carrot is the only option. Bloody feminists have a hell of a lot to answer for.

When one has served for as long as I have, cautionary yarns to tell at dinner parties are common as northerners in a mud bath. It's like having a well of anecdotes that never runs dry. Only deepening with every recruit, leave ashore, exercise or conflict.

Like the bootneck who got caught bullshitting too many times. Usually the punishment would be the 'Mad Monk' or 'Robocop' haircut, but this lad had already suffered these penalties and was *still* bullshitting his fellow bootnecks. His punishment? Ride a horse bareback through Arbroath high street. And I don't mean without a saddle. Bollock naked he galloped through the town to the bewildered amusement of the locals.

I step out into the brisk night air. The camp is eerily quiet with the only sound being my own boots on tarmac.

Then there was the bootneck who made the mistake of leaving his shower gel in the communal showers. By the time he realised his error it was too late – the bottle had been emptied. Rightfully aggrieved, he set about getting his revenge. He left another bottle in the showers the next day, this one filled with purple hair-dye. Would have been funny if we didn't have a rear admiral inspecting the camp that day. You should've seen his face at parade. It was redder than a ginger in the desert. The bulging veins on his temple the same colour as the dozen or so bootnecks stood at attention before him looking like Violet Beauregarde from *Charlie and the Chocolate Factory*.

As I pass the smoking shelter, another tale of sheer stupidity pops to mind. After finishing their cigarettes and discarding the butts down that very drain instead of in the big metal-ashtray, one bootneck thought of an easy way to earn some cash. He told his companions – only six of them – that if they each chipped in ten pounds, he'd drink a cupful of the dirty drain-water. They couldn't get their wallets out quick enough. If you discount the twenty-pound taxi-fare to bring him back from the hospital the next day, that's as honest a forty quid a bootneck will ever earn.

I reach the marine's grotts. All the rooms at the front are in darkness, but I'm no fool – if they're up to no good, drinking and the like, they'll congregate in the rooms at the rear of the building.

Another toiletry based fiasco came after a six-month deployment to Afghanistan. One bootneck was flicking through the photo's he'd taken on his newfangled digital camera. You know, reminiscing about the good times, dodging IEDs and trying not to get his head sawn off, when he stumbled across a picture he didn't recall taking. It was a photo of a big white arse with a toothbrush hanging out of it. *His* toothbrush. Fucking reprobates.

I enter the code into the door lock, and step inside the grotts.

Then there were the three bootnecks who, while in Belize for jungle-warfare training, thought it a good idea to go blindfolded into a tattooist and let the other two choose what and where they got tattooed. Yes, they're not the smartest bunch. One ended up with a tattoo below his navel that read – *IF YOU'RE READING THIS WE MUST BE RELATED.* The second got etched in German along his forearm – *YOU'VE GOT TO GIVE HITLER HIS DUES.* And the last? Well, he ended up with a caricature of the prophet who shall not be drawn on his back. No more swimming in the pool in Dubai for him.

I enter the stairwell and bound up the steps three at a time. I open the door to the first floor, peer along the corridor, and listen. Satisfied they're not here, I close the door before something of sheer stupidity catches my eye. There, above the window at the end of the landing, is a plastic bag taped to the ceiling. Fucking imbeciles. This kind of halfwitery really pisses me off.

I walk towards the offence – sniff the air like a bloodhound. Sure enough, the smell of cigarette smoke lingers. I jump and tear the bag from the ceiling revealing the smoke alarm underneath. Honestly, their folly knows no bounds. It's said if you put three bootnecks into a locked jail cell with nothing other than three cannon balls, they'd lose one, break one, and injure themselves with the last. This blatant disregard for safety alone is enough to have them running until their boots resemble a mummy's sandal. I stuff the bag into my pocket and enter the stairwell.

Not only are they bloody buffoons, they're also deviants of the highest order. A favourite 'game' of theirs is 'soggy biscuit'. The mere thought gives me the dry heave. A bunch of them stand in a circle around a biscuit placed on the ground. They each pull their plonker over the biscuit. The last one to...*finish*, has to eat said biscuit. Good luck enjoying a Mcvitie's Family Circle from now on.

I open the door to the second floor and listen. Nothing but running water coming from the heads. I creep towards it. Sure enough, there's not a soul in there, and a tap has been left on. Not only are they trying to burn the place down, they're also trying to flood it. On a plus note, at least it's more ammunition to scuttle them with. I turn the tap off and make for the stairwell.

One of the more outlandish tales of deviancy I've heard came when two bootnecks decided to spend their leave ashore in Thailand. The whole trip became a disturbed game of 'I'm more reprehensible than you', culminating when one proudly informed the other that he'd just shagged a ladyboy up the arse.

I reach the stairs and ascend to the top floor.

Not to be outdone, the second bootneck went promptly to the nearest brothel and asked for the biggest, baddest ladyboy they had...and allowed said ladyboy to shag *him* up the arse. Checkmate indeed.

I open the door, step into the top floor, and smile. Muffled music comes from the far end of the corridor. I quick-march towards it as the door opens. Out steps Marine McInnes with a mobile phone pressed against his ear. He's shirtless and unsteady – so shiters, he doesn't notice me. I stop and listen to this yappy little Jock's conversation.

He says, 'Hello?...aye...I can hear ye now...I wis too busy to answer ma phone...in Mugger's room. The wee dirty he's been smashing is in there.

She's wanting the whole lot of us to go through her...wit!? You're fuckin jokin me?' He glances up, double taking when he sees me. 'Ahh fuck. I've got eyes on. Catch ye.' He hangs up and walks towards me, doing his best to act sober. 'Sergeant *Cock*burn! Wit brings you up her—'

'It's fucking *Coe*burn!' I bellow, 'and you know very well why I'm here, Marine McInnes. Who were you speaking with on that phone?'

'Ah, c'mon now, Sergeant,' he says as he reaches me – a faux apologetic look on him. 'English isnae ma first language. Don't be racist.'

'I'll fucking racist you! You...you...you insolent bastard! Your lot kneel to the Queen of England so you'll bloody well speak her English.'

His face quickly loses all hint of apology. 'Our lot kneel for no cunt, but if ye want to get into the semantics of it, it was *us* who took *your* crown. Look up James the Sixth and the union of the crowns if yer history's no up to scratch.'

'*Marine* McInnes, I'll have you up on charge quicker than you can down a bottle of Buckfast. Now, who were you on the phone with?'

This seems to bring him to his senses. 'Em...no cunt, I mean, no one important.'

He's correct in that. Corporal Cunninghame is indeed unimportant. And a cunt. 'Not to worry, your call records will be thoroughly checked during the investigation. Now, unless you want duty weekends until your unceremonious departure, I'd suggest you start cooperating.'

He sighs deeply and puts his hands on his hips – clearly sweating neaters at my threats. 'Right, Sergeant Cockburn, I think we've got off on the wrong foot. Let's start again.'

'No need, I know *precisely* who was on the other end of that phone call. Corporal Cunninghame may be your mate, Marine McInnes, but let me be crystal clear – I am most certainly not. He's just another vagabond that needs put in his place. Sitting down in the mess telling me all is good when you lot are up here treating that uniform like it's a bloody Halloween costume. The marines that stormed Gibraltar, fought in every battle of the Napoleonic wars, and held out so valiantly against the Argies at the Falklands will be spinning in their graves. Her Majesty would be sorely disappointed to see the likes of you and Corporal Cunninghame guarding our great nation.' I shake my head. 'No wonder the sun has set on the British Empire.'

'Sarge, c'mon. Don't be like that. There's no need to—'

'It's *sergeant* and I'll be however I bloody well want to be. Now, who's in that room?'

His eyes light up and the smallest hint of a smile curls his lips. 'Well, Sergeant, I'm no gonny lie to you. There's obviously no point in tryin to fool as sharp a tool as yerself. Mugger's been riding this wee bird. Tidy wee thing with a pair of diddy's tae die for. Absolute filth, she is. Turns out she loves men in uniform. The more the merrier, if ye catch ma drift?'

'Oh, I catch your drift alright. Now, stand asid—'

'Why don't ye join us?'

'Marine McInnes, what are you suggesting?'

'Come in, let yer hair down, empty yer sack. Ye'll feel better for it, trust me.'

'Even *if* I wanted to, I couldn't. It's hardly fitting behaviour for a sergeant in Her Majesty's Royal Marines.'

'Well, I'll tell no cunt if you tell no cunt,' He says with a mischievous smirk and a wink. 'Wit d'ye say, Sergeant?'

'Em, I'm not sur—'

'C'mon, Sarge. Live a little. Don't be a plums rating – be one o' the boys.'

In a rush of blood, I almost say yes. 'No. It's out of the question. Besides, I wouldn't want my face known to some local tart. What if I'm out with the family and she recognises me?'

'We'll turn the lights oot, then.'

Am I actually considering this?

Marine McInnes grabs my arm and pulls me towards the room. 'Let's get you de-stressed.'

'Wait, wait, wait,' I say. Marine McInnes keeps dragging me along the corridor. 'I don't have any...*protection*.'

'Don't worry, Sergeant, we've got yer back.'

'No, I mean I don't have any...*contraception*.'

He stops and looks at me – a puzzled look on his face. 'Contra-wit?'

'I don't have any condoms.'

He tuts and continues his march to the room. 'Shut up, Sarge. Bone dome's are for poofters, wee lassies, and birds with moustaches. Go raw or go home.'

We reach the door as my heart feels like it's keeping time to the quick-march 'A Life on the Ocean Wave'. Marine McInnes places an index finger against his lips and signals for me to stand at the side of the door. He opens it slightly and pops his head through. Some heavy base tune wafts into the corridor, as well as...sex noises.

'Darling,' Marine Mcinnes says, 'is it awright if ma mate joins in?'

A bootneck with a heavy Scouse accent says, 'Her mouth's full but she's nodding, lad.'

Laughter leaks from the slightly ajar door.

'Wazzer!' Marine McInnes says. 'Ye're a wee gem. I'll need to turn the lights oot as he's a bit shy. That awright?'

Indiscernible mumbling before a Manc voice says, 'She says hurry up and get in. This fanny ain't gonna fuck itself.'

Marine McInnes turns to me with a beaming smile. He switches the lights off to the amusement of the occupants before opening the door wide and nodding inside. 'C'mon down...*Eddie*.'

I hesitate before he grabs my shirt and manhandles me through the door, closes it behind me.

Marine McInnes pulls me through the darkness saying, 'This way,

Eddie.'

'Who the fuck's Eddie, lad?' the Scouse voice says.

'It's a pseudonym, ya dick.' Marine McInnes says.

'What the fuck's a pseudonym?'

'Jesus fuckin Christ,' Marine McInnes says. 'Wit the fuck are they teaching yous down in Eng-ger-land-shire? Here ye go, Sarrr...Eddie!'

Laughter fills the room.

'You'd make a good sneaky beaky, lad,' the Scouser says. 'Fucking double-O-silly-cunt.'

'Get it round ye, ya house-breaking bastard,' Marine McInnes says, pushing me forward.

I stumble against what feels like a bed. My flailing arms touch bare skin. Thankfully, the silky softness tells me it's female. I fumble in the dark. An arm, shoulder, head that's moving to and fro, the pertiest breast I've ever felt. My elbow brushes against someone standing next to me.

'She's all yours...*Eddie*,' a Geordie voice says right next to my ear before moving away.

Next thing I'm being grabbed at as my belt gets ripped off.

My johnson's harder than the Royal Marines selection test.

Warm hands pull my trousers and underwear down before grabbing my...throbbing member.

My stomach goes that fluttery way when you crest a steep hill in your car when her tongue tickles my prince-albert.

She hungrily takes the lot in her mouth.

My god. This feels *so* hoofing.

Shit. The beginnings of an orgasm are building. I sure as hell won't empty my clip so quickly in front of the bootnecks. I withdraw, push her back onto the bed, grab her thighs, and pull her arse towards the end of the bed.

She lets out a moan as I enter her.

I'm praying her sodden minge is from her own bodily fluids as I pound away. Unlike the Jocks, I do not enjoy stirring porridge. Particularly if it's another man's.

The boys are saying, 'Go on, Eddie,' and 'Give it rice, Eddie.'

I'm pounding away like a rabbit on a jackhammer.

She's moaning – her warm breath fills my ear.

Before long, that tickly feeling begins deep within my crown jewels.

There's no holding this one back as my pumping becomes deep and slow – holding for maximum pleasure.

She senses it coming and arches her back, pushing against my lower abdomen.

'Rule Bri-fucking-tania!' I shout as I cum with all the explosive force of a hellfire missile.

My heart skips a beat as the lights come on to cheers and whistles.

I'm nose to nose, looking into her green eyes.

Dear god, no.

My world collapses, and I jump up and out her with a squelch.

Those familiar green eyes fill with shock as she scurries up to the top end of the bed.

I cup my hands over my mouth as I wretch and gag at the putrid bile scalding my throat.

She pulls her knees up to her chest and manages a single, exasperated word.

'Dad!'

THE GREAT DIVIDER

(Opening of Upcoming Novel)

Well bro, even though ah've never been scared ay dyin, ma heart quickens an stomach churns the moment ah step ontae the pier wall. Apart fae the lappin waves far below, the harbour's quieter than a politician's conscience.

The Harbour Inn's rowdiness barred behind metal shutters. Nae auld dears gettin in their early mornin walk n natter. Nae workies sittin alone in their van, eatin their takeaway lunch fae Steamers Cafe, n wistfully gazin oot tae sea. No even a single one ay they eternal optimists, casting a line oafy the dock.

The harbour's so still at this hour, ye maybe even be able tae hear ghosts of the past. And if ye liten, *really* listen, ye might even learn a thing or two fae they ghosts before their whispered warnings become lost on the vast ocean of time. The sun's nonchalantly rising, as it's known tae do, on another insignificant moment that feels so important tae everyone livin it.

Ah fuck wae ma in-built systems ay self preservation, n shuffle forward so's only ma heels are keepin us tethered tae the pier wall. Ah totally get why folk go on rollercoasters or jump outta planes or pump their sister-in-law. The closer ye are tae death, the more alive ye feel. And in this moment, ah'm Doctor Frankenstein's beautiful monster.

Ye see, most folk urnae *actually* scared ay dying. No really. They're scared ay livin. *Really* livin. Frozen in perpetual impotence at the limitless potential within.

A wise ghost fae the past once said, 'It is not death that a man should fear, but he should fear never beginning to live.'

That gendered language might be considered 'problematic' by today's virtuous standards, but it doesnae make it any less true. And in that unimaginably lonesome moment when death's icy breath chills yer neck, n vice-like grip is clamped ontae yer shoulder, the stark realisation hits that it's no fear of the unknown beyond that terrifies ye. No. It's the known truth that ye squandered the pitiful time ye had, worrying n fussing over things that mean not a jot.

Making sure yer bins are out in time.

Marvelling at how much weight the current in-fashion celebrity has lost on their new diet.

Bemoanin yer weak wifi signal when sittin in yer hot tub.

Consumin yer daily dose ay fear-porn fae the corporate masters, and fretting over whatever the latest existential threat they tell you is.

Having tae wait a whole hour for the meal ye ordered on a phone that has more technology than the Apollo crafts, n was made by child slaves.

Sweating that a word or phrase you've typed in an email might hurt the precious feelings of a work colleague who ye wouldnae spend one minute wae if ye wurnae gettin paid.

Unleashing yer pent up frustrations on those closest tae ye when yer pishy sportsball team loses.

Wonderin why yer ungrateful weans that – through no choice of their own – YOU fuckin brought intae existence, aren't living up tae YOUR high standards. Then spittin the dummy when they fling ye in an old-folks home and forget about ye.

However ye choose tae distract yerself, there comes a point when that wee voice ye've been suppressing can no longer be ignored. And like the inevitable trip tae the vet when yer auld dug starts draggin its hind legs, that reckoning comes for us all. Unfortunately, that moment comes far too late for far too many.

Ah take a lungful ay fresh sea-air and exhale through pursed lips. Who woulda thought Malky Cunninghame would be considerin this? If ye'd told us that a month ago, ah would've laughed in yer face an telt ye no tae be such a stupid cunt.

Ye see, lifes a series ay choices, and we're the sum ay they choices.

Have the cake or the carrot.

The decaffeinated or full buzz.

Mindlessly scroll through yer phone or read a book.

Spin a web ay deceit or speak the truth.

See red n fly up the arse ay the driver that's just cut ye up, or smile n back aff.

Bang yer new, tidy-as-fuck workmate, or go home tae yer well-worn spouse.

Stick the heed oan the steamer that's joost barged intae ye, or laugh n walk away.

Write a catty reply tae the clown that posted somethin ye oppose, or listen tae them in the hope ye may become wiser.

Swallow a bullet or soldier on.

Sounds easy, no?

A seagull lands beside us, squawkin and lookin at us querly. It shuffles toward us.

Feed the hungry Gannett or volley the rat-wae-wings.

Wit would you do?

Even noo, standin on the edge wae nothin but air between us n the choppy water below, ah've still got two choices at hand.

How in the fuck *did* it come tae this?

You guessed it – choices. Ma own decisions have led us here. Granted, the past few weeks have been mental – even by ma standards – but ah've no cunt tae thank but maself. And, in ma thirty-three years oan this fucked up excuse of a world, this is by *far*, the biggest decision ah've had tae make.

* * *

· Take a large helping of nihilism.
· Stir into a hollow, desiccated, consumer society.
· Mix one part disappearing jobs with one part meaningless jobs.
· Douse with ego-infused, narcissistic sauce.
· Sprinkle in a form of communication that runs the grain of millions of years of evolution.
· Whisk two parts opposing ideologies – dealer's choice.
· Sieve out and discard the truth.
· Simmer over a broken and barren, suicidal civilisation.
· Turn the heat of wealth disparity to gas mark six and bring to the boil.
· Serve with as much alcohol as your liver can take.

Voila! Malky's Madras. Guaranteed tae water yer eyes.

* * *

BEEP BEEP BEEEEP!

The cold water's refreshin as it rinses the shaving foam from ma face. Never been one for facial hair. When every other cunt wis jumpin on the beard-growin bandwagon, ah kept ma face smoother than a baby-oiled tit. Besides, this badge ay honour runnin fae ear tae chin deserves prominent showcase. It's the ultimate status symbol for a top boy of one ay the most feared young teams there was. Ah'm a big believer in eye contact. No cunt can hold ma gaze when they've got this scar screamin for attention. Every deep, reddened inch of it wis earned, n ah walk around wae it full ay pride. The cunt that gave us it doesnae walk at all. Well, no withoot a heavy limp at least.

The young team days are long gone, but ah still look relatively fresh-faced. A full head ay dirty-blonde hair wae no a single grey in sight, helps. It's funny how it's the cunts goin bald that bleat oan about men ageing gracefully. Bullshit. That's one ay the many lies they tell theirselves so's they can look in the mirror withoot wantin tae open their wrists intae the sink.

Ah douse some aftershave on, skoosh some deodorant ontae ma oxters, n head intae the kitchen.

BEEP BEEP BEEE—

Ah open the microwave n take out the defrosted chicken breasts, give them a sniff tae make sure. Ah stick the wok ontae the hob n fire it up. The big kitchen knife feels right at home as ah dice the chicken. Ah'm always Hank Marvin after a good night out, but wouldnae touch the shite they shovel up at they venues. Or takeaway places for that matter. Ah know fae experience that these cunts have no qualms aboot paddin out their meals wae all sorts.

When ah wis a boy, ah used tae go fishin doon the harbour. Absolute dunkies ah spent there during one school holiday catching fuck-all but the cauld. Didnae help that ah had an auld shitey rod wae a fucked reel that ah found in a skip. The first few times ah don't even think ah used floats or baited the hook. Just flung the line in and hoped for the best. That's wit happens when ye've nae father tae show ye these things. Ye fuck up then give up. That's exactly wit ah did. Ah remember walkin home fae the third or fourth day spent wastin ma time absolutely ragin.

As ah passed the Harbour Inn, a familiar voice said, 'Any joy the day, wee man?'

Ah turned – ma big brother's pal Zander walked out the boozer. Ah don't know if ma brother wis inside as ah wisnae exactly in the mood for chattin. That would've depended on his status wae the landlord at the time. Ma money's on him being barred. Zander wis sound, always giving us a couple ay quid n that, but ah wisnae wantin any cunt tae know about yet another failure, so ah kept walkin.

'Where's yer rod?' he shouted.

'In the fuckin bin,' ah said, before runnin away.

The wok sizzles n spits when ah scrape half ay the diced chicken intae it. Ah put the rest in a tub, and stick it in the fridge before stirring the pan.

The mornin after givin up on the fishin, ma bedroom door gets booted in before the sun's even up.

'Drop yer cocks n grab yer socks,' ma brother said.

Ah remember tellin him tae get tae fuck, n pullin the covers over ma head. He ripped the quilt aff ay ma bed, skipping away fae ma kicks. Ah roared at him tae give us it back.

'Ye can have one thing,' he said. 'This.' He held up ma fusty batman quilt. 'Or this.' He held up a black case, like wit folk carry guns in but longer.

Ma eyes must've lit up. 'Is that a...?'

'Brand new, top-ay-the-range, all singin, all dancin, undamaged fae its fall aff the back ay a lorry, fishin rod,' he said, aw smug.

The beaming smile that crossed ma face must've told him exactly wit ma choice was.

He flung it at us n said, 'Ye've ten minutes tae get ready or ah'm oot the door withoot ye. I'll no be missin the early worm.'

No knowin the meanin ay that saying, ah thought we were goin tae dig for worms, but he'd already got some. As well as everythin else a buddin fisherman needs – floats, anchors, a net, n best of all, a big, fuck-off Rambo-knife. 'Just in case a shark tries tae fuck wae us,' he said.

And by the way, that blade *did* save us fae a few sharks over the years. Just no the marine kind.

He'd even made us chopped-pork rolls n packed ma favourite munchies – Bikers crisps n Taz bars. Wit a day that wis. Sittin wae ma legs hangin over the pier, listenin tae ma big brother's stories. And let me tell you, he had a few. I'd heard whisperings about him, n it seemed the polis were always at the door for him, but ah think that wis the first time ah'd actually heard it fae the horse's mouth. Now, ah'm sure he gave us the watered doon version, but still, some ay the things he got up tae would've put the Devil tae shame.

He even told us something no one else knew – that he'd enlisted tae join the Royal Marines. If only ah knew then...

Ah grab an onion n some peppers fae the fridge, chop them up n fire them intae the wok. The spices n hot-sauce singe ma nostrils when added tae the mixture.

Hand on heart, that day fishin wae ma brother wis one ay the best days ay ma shite life. We never even caught any fish. We did, however, catch quite a few eels. Long, black, slippery things that were murder tae unhook. One even slipped fae ma brother's grasp n back intae the sea as he swung it doon tae smash its head against the ground. Lucky bastard. Ah thought we were taking them home tae cook up. Ah remember askin if they tasted any good.

He laughed. 'Only if ye don't know yer eatin them.' Then he told us the plan. 'Take these up the toon n go tae all the takeaways. Some will chase ye, but others will pay for them. Back in ma day, the Jade Dragon paid best, but go round them all n see who offers ye the most. Let them know yer hawking them tae every other restaurant, n the highest bidder gets them. So's they don't try and rip ye aff.'

And that's exactly wit ah did. Our wee fishing days turned intae a regular thing. As well as being a good wee earner for a primary-school wean that rarely got any pocket money. God knows how many cunts over the years thought they were tucking intae chicken curry. Little did they know, it wis the Cunninghame brothers eels!

That's why ah don't do takeaways.

Fuck, ah know cunts that laced bread wae rat poison n fed it tae the birds. Bagsful ay dead pigeons n seagulls they used tae flog tae them. The sick bastards. Never could bring maself tae do that. Killin fish is one thing, but birds? They've too much emotion in their piercing, knowing eyes. Some folk don't like these 'rats wae wings'. Ah say they're just tryin tae survive like the rest of us.

That reminds us.

Ah open the bread bin, take out the dregs, and fling them oot the backdoor. By the time ah turn aff the hob, pour ma scran intae a plastic tub tae cool, n go tae the sink, a flock ay six birds have settled in tae dine. Ah watch them as ah'm washin the dishes. Four crows n two magpies. Wit's that sayin again? One for sorrow, two for joy? Dancer! Must be ma lucky day. As ah sit the wok on the drainin board, a big bastard seagull wae a gammy leg swoops in, scatterin the smaller birds. That's survival ay the fittest right there.

Ah head intae ma bedroom n rake through ma wardrobe. Nothing too flamboyant for the night. Ah pull oot ma white, oxford shirt. This'll complement ma black jeans n jacket just fine. As ah'm buttonin it up, the pre-night-jitters begin tae buzz – ma tits are well and truly jacked. All going tae plan, the adrenaline will be surging through us like a toddler that's just stuck it's finger in a socket, and ah'll be shakin like Michael J. Fox on a trampoline during an earthquake at the North Pole. Can not wait. This night's been months in the making, n ah'll be an unhappy camper if ma toil wis all for nothin. Shouldnae come tae that, though. There's no such thing as a sure bet in this life, but this scenario is as close as can be. Ah fling ma jacket on n bounce oot tae do wit ah do best.

* * *

VROOOM

Ma mobile connects tae the car stereo. Ah select the 'Music For You' playlist. Let's see wit the AI says ma taste in music is. The pounding drum-beat intro of Oasis's 'Bring It On Down' reverberates around ma motor, uplifts this dark heart within. Good start, Skynet. Good start. The windscreen wipers turn on as ah'm pullin away.

It's only spittin, but the pressing, grey clouds overhead threaten. They're so low, the wheels ay a jumbo jet would smash intae the tops ay buildings if it tried flying below them. Summertime in Scotland. Canny whack it. No wonder everycunt's depressed. No me, though. Ma number one rule is — if ye let the weather stop ye in this country, ye'd get fuck-all done. Ah often wonder wit the hunter-gatherers that first stepped foot here were thinkin. They must've been right sadistic cunts tae settle a land that would sooner torture than nurture.

The venue's a couple ay towns over. A twenty-minute drive for most cunts. But ah'm no most cunts. It's the scenic route for me. Everycunt's in a rush these days. Ye can see the stress on their faces as they whizz about like flies in a jam jar. The perception ay getting somewhere distracts them fae the fact they're goin nowhere.

Ah turn ontae the back roads as the heavens open. Liam Gallagher's searing voice is replaced by Meatloaf's rangy one as 'Life Is A lemon' blares. Rollin green hills stretch intae the distance. Ah open the window n take a lung full ay fresh, country air. Some folk don't like this dung-filled air. I'd take it over the piss perfumed schemes any day.

It's no long before a motor flies up ma arse. A guy in a shitbox people-carrier. He's bealin at the cunt in front who's driving so slow. Ah lift ma foot off the accelerator. The cunt gets closer. He shakes his head, aw exaggerated, making sure ah see that he's pissed. Ah smile n laugh, hoping he can see us through the rear-view mirror. He does n throws his arms up.

Better keep hold ay that steerin wheel, pal, in case you need tae brake suddenly.

We round a sharp bend. The road straightens, stretchin far intae the distance. There's no oncomin motors. This is yer chance, pal. He has a look. And another. Do it. Third time lucky as he pulls oot like a good Catholic. His engine roars as he draps gears n floors it.

Ah let him pull alongside. He's glarin at us, giving us the daggers. Ah press the accelerator and match his speed. He flips oot. Between glances ahead, he's pointin and shoutin. Fuck knows wit he's saying, but his face tells us all ah need tae know. The bend ahead is fast approaching. Ah look him in the eye, smile, n give him the hitchhiker's thumb. He does as commanded n pulls in behind – barely a bawhair's width between our bumpers.

He leans on the horn, flashes his headlights, n gives us the wanker sign.

Is that right? Let's see who the wanker is.

We round the bend – the road's still empty. Ah drift over the centre line n slow down gradually, bringing us tae a stop before bouncin oot ma motor.

His face draps. There's nowhere tae go, and he knows it.

Ah saunter towards him.

His eyes dart between his rear view mirrors.

Ah reach the front ay his motor as he crunches intae reverse n whines away. Ah keep walking as his back end turns, bumps ontae the grass verge. He slams intae first n spins away, tearin his rear bumper aff on the verge.

So predictable. Everycunt's a hard-case in the sanctuary ay their motor or behind a computer screen. It's like ma brother used tae say – most cunts shite it when ye face them down.

A horn blasts behind us. Ah turn. A wee red motor's sittin the other side ay ma own, unable tae pass. The horn blasts again. Let's see if this road warrior's got bigger balls than the last. Ah stride towards it, glaring at the driver. Just as ah reach ma motor, the driver's window lowers. A bald, wrinkled, pensioner's head pokes out like a tortoise fae its shell.

Fuck.

'Wit you playin at?' he shouts.

Ah hold up ma hands. 'Sorry, pal, ah wis just—'

'Get it shifted!'

Wide auld cunt. Lucky he's no twenty years younger. 'Will do, pal.'

Ah jump back in ma motor. Emimem's now waxin lyrical about how he still doesnae give a fuck. The auld wideo gives us the evils as ah drive away. Clearly he's aff the same mould as young Marshall.

After renditions ay The Jam's 'Going Underground', Queens 'Headlong', Sweet's 'Ballroom Blitz', Jamie T's 'Sticks n Stones', OCS's 'The Riverboat Song', and Pulp's 'Common People', ah roll intae town like an outlaw fae an old western. The rain's cleared n the sun's splitting the sky – steam rises fae the sodden tarmac. Only in Scotland. Wouldnae be surprised tae see snow next.

The Arctic Monkeys 'A Certain Romance' fires up. A fittin anthem for a town once described in a travel mag as '...an industrial backwater with a violent reputation...' Only, all the industries have done a bunk, so wit does that make it now? This place used tae be a quaint little toon before the powers that be did wit they do best and fucked shit up. Doubt if the folk ay this toon had any say in the matter when it was chosen to house the dregs from the city's post-war slums clearances. All that achieved wis movin the problem ontae some other cunts shoulders. Like when the Catholic Church moved paedo priests. Some unsuspecting parish would be changed beyond recognition. That's the way of us – let some other cunt deal wae it. Plasters for severed spines should be humanity's motto.

Ah turn left n pull the visor down. At least the sun still shines in hell. A couple ay youngsters keek out fae a lane just along fae an off-licence. As ah drive past, the rest ay the troops are further up the lane. Time for ma good deed ay the day. Ah spin around at the next junction n head back tae the shop. After fillin ma boot wae an alkies wet dream – a case ay super-strength lager, three big bottles ay cider, five bottles ay tonic wine – ah head for the lane. The young team growls at us as ah'm reversin intae it.

Ah pop the boot, open ma window, n turn the music doon. 'Christmas has come early, boys.'

They're silent, apprehensive even, as they move closer. 'Fuck me,' one says, 'it's full ay swally.'

There's excited chatter before one swaggers tae ma window. A wee guy decked oot in a tracky that would've cost as much as a decent suit. He's got aw the front ay a Jack Russel.

'Is that for us?' he says.

Ah nod.

'It aw?'

'Every. Last. Drop.'

'Fuckin belter! Grab the lot, troops. How much do we owe ye, big man?' One ay his big pals joins him, pulls oot a wad ay notes. He must be the Rottweiler tae the wee man's Jack Russel.

'Wit dae they call yous?' ah ask.

'TMS,' the bold Jack says.

Ahh, the Toonbridge Mad Sqwad. 'Never heard ay yeez.'

He throws his head back n laughs. 'Fuck sake, mate. We're the most feared young team there is.'

Ha! This wee guy's got more neck than ET sittin on a giraffe. Typical wee man syndrome. 'Who do yous fight?'

He straightens his cap. 'No cunts got the baws tae fight us.'

'Who dae yeez chase then?'

'Anycunt that comes round here thinkin they're a ticket.'

Fuck me. This wee guy should be a politician the way he's dodgin ma questions. Ah'm tempted tae jump oot n start acting like the biggest ticket there is. See if their bullshit is bravado or no.

Ah look him in the eye. 'Listen, *wee* man. I'll ask again, n if ah don't get a straight answer, I'll bounce oot this motor, slap every single one ay yeez aboot, take ma drink back, n give it tae the next young team ah see. Now...Who. Do. Yous. Fight?'

He's stunned for a moment before his eyes narrow n lips curl intae a sneer. He opens his mouth, but his big pal behind beats him tae the punch.

'It's the Castlebank TOI.'

'Thank you,' ah say, without takin ma eyes fae Jack. 'Now, as long as ye promise that some ay they bottles will be gettin put over the heads ay the Castlebank TOI, ye can keep yer money n go buy some drugs. Deal?'

Wee Jack doesnae answer. He's raging, and just choking tae put one on us. But he's also choking for some bevvy. Now there's a tougher choice than Sophie had.

'Deal?' ah say.

His big pal nudges him. He begrudgingly nods.

'Thank you.'

Ah drive away. Wee Jack stands there glaring. Ah don't know wit's runnin through his mind, but ah'm willing tae bet he'll be smashin some poor cunt the night while picturin it's me. Ah smile, hit the accelerator, n turn the volume up. The Kaiser Chiefs are belting oot their predictions for a riot. Ah'm inclined tae agree.

The mass of 'To Let' signs, bookies, boozers, takeaways, n charity shops tells us ah'm on the high-street. It's just like every other toon centre – dying on its arse. Nearly there, though. Ah grip the steerin wheel in anticipation – sweat's moistened ma palms.

The melodic intro tae Queen's 'The Great Pretender' blares fae the speakers.

'Ya beauty!' ah fuckin love this song. Nothing but full-belt will do.

'Oh yes! I'm the great, divider (ooh ooh)
Diviiiding the world, pretty well (ooh ooh)
my neeeed is such, ah diviiide, like the church
ah'm ecstatic, but no cunt, can tell.

'Ohh yes! I'm the great, divider (ooh ohh)
Ruuunnin a world, doused in flames (ooh ooh)
ah ruuun the game, but to my, real shame
You've left me, to divide, all alone.

'Too real, is this feeling, of make (make!) believe
Too real, when ah feel, what my heart, can't conceal
Ohh wow yes! ah'm the great, divider (ooh ohh)
Diviiiding the world, fae ma phone

I seeem to be, what ah'm not (you see)
ah'm wearing, ma heart, like a broken bone
Pretending, that you're, still around
Yeeeeeaah! Woo-hoo!'.

Ah park round the corner fae the venue. Ma pulse quickens n I've got a nudger on as ah stride through the car park. The front ay the Victorian, sandstone buildin is buzzin wae smokers, vapers, n tagalongs. They congregate around the new glass extension. Somebody thought it a good idea tae modernise this beautiful buildin. Fuckin arsehole.

Ah reach the automatic doors. A steamer, looking like the type ay cunt you'd find puntin gear fae the back ay a scooter in Ibiza, staggers oot, announcing, 'Call the cops, ah'm oot ma chops!'

Ah smile n step inside. The cops will be here soon, ma mucker. The cops will be here soon.

* * *

Malky's Idiot-proof Guide to a Cracking Night Out

Step One:
Find a healthy rivalry that can be nursed into something more hostile. A white-collar boxing match where one fighter is off the Gypsies, and the other is off the Bikers should do.

Step Two:
Nail your colours to the mast. This can be done by setting up two

fake accounts across unsocial media. One for each side. For example –
bikerboy666 and travellerman69.

Step Three:

Get in with the respective tribes. Some praising comments showing
your support will do. *'The next King of the Gypsies!'* and *'Mate, your hands
move like a bat out of hell!'*. They'll lap that kinda arse-kissing stuff right
up.

Step Four:

Wind up the other side. Doesn't take much. A few snide comments
under a video of their boy training will stoke the flames of hostility. *'Ha!
Stick to laying tarmac and robbing pensioners, you pikey cunt.'* and *'Fuck
me, this biker's so useless, he'll need to trade in his Harley for a mobility
scooter by the time our boy's finished with him.'* Obviously, the closer to
the bone, the better.

Step Five:

Gradually increase the prods until it's unbridled contempt you're
unleashing. Don't worry, they'll gladly match you. Keep this going all
the way to the big night. Just before the bell rings, let each side know
that their boy's a pussy and he's gonny get smashed and so will the lot
of them if they've got something to say about it.

Step Six:

Sit back and enjoy the fireworks. Or, if you're more like me, wade in
and get yourself burnt.

* * *

'SWEEEEEET CA-RO-LINE, OH! OH! OH!'

The cavernous grand-hall is bouncin. Like a train bound for Auschwitz, it's standin room only. From the balcony tae ringside, everycunt's on their feet, singin n clappin. The sweat n testosterone hanging so thick, ye can taste it wae yer colon. Unlike some ay the previous bouts, not a single cunt's lookin at their phone. All eyes are on the stage at the far side ay the ring, eagerly anticipating the ring walk. Some ay the previous boxers were piss-poor. Plenty ay heart but no technique. Such is the way at unsanctioned boxin shows.

The lights dim n the music stops. A spotlight shines ontae the ring. The dinner-suited announcer taps the microphone n holds it below his mouth.

'Lllladies and Gentlemeeeen! Are! You! Jacked!?'

The crowd roars, showing their jacked-to-the-fucking-tits.

'After some top-notch bouts, the moment you've all been waiting for has arrived.'

The crowd agrees with all the enthusiasm of a coked-up virgin at a brothel.

'This is the big one, the grudge match, and, if the lead up to tonight is anything to go by, it won't leave you disappointed. So, without further ado, please give a rousing welcome to the FIGHTERS!'

The marionettes near lift the roof oafy the buildin.

'First to enter the ring. Fighting out of Elite Boxing Gym. He's the Gorilla from Gateside, riding via the gates of hell itself! Satan's sidekick...MARK! THE MONKEY! MCKIE!'

ACDC'S 'Highway to Hell' begins. Spotlights race around the hall. Ah roll ma eyes at this mainstream rock that would have real bikers turnin in their patches in disgust. The ones here seem tae enjoy it as the entire right-hand side of the ring erupts. Then again, most music sounds good when yer pished.

The boy makes his way tae the ring. Half the hall cheer, while the other half jeer. He doesnae seem tae notice as he steps intae the ring, and side steps around it with his hands raised. It's clear how he got his ring name – he's hairier than Susan Boyle's bath plughole. He finally acknowledges his support when they chant his name.

The music stops, the spotlights dim.

'His opponent tonight,' says the announcer.

The Bikers boo while the Gypsies clap n whistle.

'Fighting out of Hurricane Hands Boxing Club. He's the bare-knuckle champ of the north, old shovel-hands himself! The Grave Digger...CHRISIE! GOLDEN GLOVES! GILLESPIE!'

I'll need tae remember n thank this announcer. He's doin us a solid in gettin these clowns wound up.

DJ Fresh's 'Goldust' blares. His support massed on the left-hand side approves as they bounce up n doon like leprechauns on hot coals. This'll likely still be in the top ten ay the Gypsy hit-parade. They cheer their boy, clearly tryin tae outdo the Bikers, as he bounds towards the ring. He's got the game face on and is near sprintin.

He vaults the tap rope n makes a beeline for the enemy. The biker boy steps towards him as the ref jumps in between. The two stand squared off, head n shoulders above the ref who's tryin tae get them intae their corners. The wee ref gets roundly ignored as they shout n gesture at each other before their corner men drag them away. This electrifies the crowd.

Ah rub ma hands together. This is shapin up nicely. Ah cannot *wait* tae see wit happens when *Sons of Anarchy* n *Snatch* collide. Ah send out ma final baited messages n sit back tae enjoy the entertainment.

Tae tell the truth, ah'm no really a sporty guy. It's more the rivalry that appeals. Especially if it's a deep-rooted one involvin some ideology ah can nurture – religion, politics, nationalism. Ah actually like referees. Well, it's more jealousy. These cunts get tae piss off both sides with impunity. Lucky bastards.

Ma phone's thrummin away in ma pocket like a cam-girl on speed. Wonder how many here are biting. It's amazing how easy it's become tae trigger the monkey brain these days. And in a room packed wae boozed-up Gypsies n Bikers, there's more monkey brains than at a Chinese wet market.

After official introductions, the ref brings them tae the centre for the pre-bout talk. They're no listenin. They'll likely be picturin rippin the others heed aff, n drop-kicking it intae their support. Their supporters are gettin in on the act. They're pointing n shouting at each other. Tribalism at its finest.

No matter wit the tree-pumpin hippies say, it's in oor blood. We're a tribal species, n ah wis born in the most tribal places of them all – bonny Scotland. From the patchwork ay Celtic tribes that loved nothin better than knockin the shite outta each other – till they Roman bastards rocked up, compelling them tae join forces – tae the Highland Clans and Border Reivers, right uptae the sectarian divide that began over three centuries ago and is still thriving today.

Fuck, when ah wis a boy, our gang battled any n all other young team's in oor toon. Until some wideo's fae somewhere else stopped by. Then we'd team up wae oor toonsfolk n go right ahead wae the interlopers. When we were abroad n cunts fae other countries were gettin wide – usually the English – we'd team up wae any other Scots n get tore right in aboot them. If world war three broke out the morra, ah'm sure we'd drap any grudge wae the English, and stand alongside them against whoever that new threat was. Those cunts we happily slaughtered, be they terrorists, communists or fascists – fucked if ah know wit differentiates these cunty tribes – would quickly become our best pals if ET decided tae come back mob-handed. As soon as we sent they bug-eyed pricks packin it'd be back tae square-going each other. Tribalism is the glue that binds us as a species.

DING DING

The combatants belt fae their corners, clash in the middle like rutting stags on coke.

The crowds on their feet, roaring their boy on.

The fighters rain hooks, haymakers, n over-hands at the other before clinching. The ref steps in, separates the pair. The Gypsy hooks his leg around the Biker's n throws him tae the ground.

The watchin Gypsies cheer while the Bikers boo. Half ay them are spending more time locked eyes wae the opposing fans.

The ref gives the Gypsy a warnin. He's no givin a fuck. He's one thing on his mind. The ref signals for them tae fight.

The Gypsy steams in, telegraphing an overhand right.

The Biker ducks underneath, pivots on his left fit, and comes up wae an absolutely beautiful left hook.

It's now the Bikers turn tae cheer n deride the opposition as the Gypsy hits the deck.

'*ONE. TWO.*'

Ah slide back fae the chair's edge n take a breath. Wit a fuckin start.

'*FIVE. SIX.*'

The Gypsie's struggling tae his feet – his supporters willing him up.

'*NINE.*'

He makes it. The ref gives him the once over before signalling tae continue.

It's Biker boy's turn tae steam in. He gets his opponent against the ropes n opens up.

The Gypsie's coverin as best he can, but the Biker's teeing aff him.

The Gypsie's corner men are shoutin at him tae clinch.

The refs havin a good look. Don't see this going much longer.

The ten-second clapper sounds, and the Gypsy pushes the Biker away.

The moment the Biker closes the distance, the Gypsy opens up wae a wild right. The lucky bastard catches him square on the jaw, sending the Biker crashin tae the canvas.

The Biker's supporters put hands on heads as the Gypsies explode.

Biker boy doesnae look too fucked – he gets straight up as the bell rings.

The entire hall erupts, showin their approval at two minutes of absolute beautiful brutality.

Jesus fuckin Christ. That wis an absolute *war* of a first round. They fought like Sunni n Shia, held fuck all back. Four more ay this'll do nicely.

The remainin rounds flew in, and were every bit as entertaining as the first. Each ay them scored another knockdown, fought like absolute warriors, n left everythin out there. Clearly spent, the pair wait in their corners for the decision. This'll be a difficult choice.

The crowd's on their feet. Nervous energy hangs in the air like shame on a porn set after a fifty-man, bukkake gang-bang. Four black-polo-shirted bouncers guard each side ay the ring.

Time for me tae move fae ma neutral position, but which side tae choose? The Gypsy showed more aggression, but the Biker wis the more technical fighter. It really is eachy-peachy. Ah make ma way tae the back ay the bikers support as the bell rings and announcer taps his mic.

The crowd falls silent. The two warriors join in the middle, embrace, and stand either side of the ref.

Fuck. These cunts better no be thinking they're pals now.

The announcer steps forward, a look of incredulity etched across his face. *'Ladies and gentlemen. What! Did! I! Tell you!'*

The crowd cheers in response.

'That was a truly epic contest, and leaves no doubt as to what the fight of the night is.'

Fight ay the night so far.

'Please, put your hands together and show your appreciation for these two warriors.'

Like imprisoned sea lions, the crowd dutifully applauds. The two fighters do the same before embracin again.

Not good. The hostility between the two, and their supporters, has been replaced by respect.

'So, after five hard fought rounds, we go to the scorecards.'

It goes so quiet ye could hear a mouse yodel.

'The cards are in, and we have a unanimous decision.'

There's a collective inhale that nearly drains the hall ay oxygen.

'All three judges score the bout...' He glances at the score-cards, lettin the tension linger for a moment longer. *'...46 to 46. A draw!'*

Shitebag cunts.

The crowd applauds. The ref thrusts the pair's hands in the air. The useless bastards embrace again.

This won't do.

Each fighter goes tae the opposin fans n applauds them – they return the gesture.

This won't do at all. The flames ay hostility ah'd worked so hard tae fan are being pissed on before ma eyes.

Fuck this for a game ay soldiers.

An empty beer bottle lies at ma feet. Ah glance around. All eyes are on the ring n there's no cunt behind us.

Time tae get this fire started.

Ah grab the bottle, give another quick check, n launch it wae all ma might.

The kindling soars above the bikers, over the ring, lands among the Gypsies, n bursts intae flames in the form ay screamin.

Like meerkats on the Serengeti, everycunt instinctively looks at the source ay the screams.

A blonde-haired woman among the Gypsies is fussin over a wean next tae her. That wean's head is covered in blood.

Who the fuck brings a wean tae a boxing show?

A crowd ay Gypsies have surrounded the screamin wean n enraged woman. She's rantin, 'The dirty bastards! They've bottled ma wean!'

The Bikers glance at each other wae puzzled faces.

The Gypsies shout n point, some ay them are being held back. A bottle soars fae among them, lands impotently among the Bikers, smashing on the ground.

It's now the Bikers turn tae up hostilities.

Ah smile as the adrenaline begins tae flow. It's like ma brother used tae say – stupidity spreads faster than any virus ever could.

A couple ay Gypsies have made their way around the side ay the ring, but they're blocked by the security.

C'mon lads, pass this barrier.

There's shouts of, 'NAW! JOHN-JOE, NAW!'

One ay the Gypsies has scrambled intae the ring. He beelines tae the far side n launches two bottles intae the Bikers point-blank.

Go on yerself, John-Joe.

The Bikers roar. The security wall's breached. Chairs n bottles fly like Wall Street cunts on 9/11. The Gypsy vanguard clashes at the corner wae a group ay Bikers. More Gypsies flood the ring. One launches himself fae the top rope like the Heartbreak Kid – the Jawbreak Kid, we'll call him. He's grabbed tae the ground n disappears under a maelstrom ay angry Bikers. Some ay the Bikers attempt tae storm the ring. A series ay head kicks repels them. The Gypsies won't give up the high ground easily. The two boxers n their corners begin round six. The ref n announcer scarper.

This symphony ay violence crescendos beautifully as ma nudger goes full-blown raging hardon. This must've been how Dr Frankenstein felt watching his labour ay love, his monstrous creation, his baby come tae life.

Now, when this sorta malarkey occurs, there's three kinds ay folk – flighters, freezers, n fighters. The biggest group – the flighters – get the hell outta Dodge. The next biggest group is the freezers. They stand there like they've just locked eyes wae the Medusa, clutchin their hearts or cuppin their hands over horrified faces. Clearly shocked, but no enough tae warrant the flight mechanism. The last group – the fighters, folk off ma own back – wade in, clearly infused wae the mayhem. Among them are the bouncers.

Six ay them gather at the main entrance, the hesitancy reeking fae them as the flighters surge past. Their white-shirted supervisor joins them, waves his tattooed arms about while barking a pre-battle speech William Wallace would've been proud of, before turnin n leadin them flying-V style intae the melee.

The spectacle enthuses us, n ah'm foamin at the zip. This must be how a junkie feels watchin his pal cook up. Ah slip ma jacket oaf n let it fall tae the ground. Time for us tae shoot up.

Ah get tore in like the Tasmanian Devil, flinging digs at everycunt. Big or wee, black or white, able-bodied or crippl—ye get the point. They're all gettin it. Anycunt within arms reach of a punch, legs reach of a kick, or throws reach of a chair. Now *there's* equality for ye.

Ah'm at the ring. Two hairy-arsed Bikers have a skinny wee Gypsy on the ground, bootin the absolute shite outta him. Ah smash a chair across one, n lay the other oot wae a right.

The Gypsy staggers tae his feet. 'Cheers the now, frien—'

BOOM!

His nose shatters when ma forehead lands flush, sending him back doon.

Ah step over him, searching for the next target.

The head bouncer looks promisin. He's in the thick ay it, battin away anycunt that gets close like the faither in the end scene ay *The Wanderers*.

Target acquired.

Ah head straight for him, steppin over a carpet ay broken bottles, mangled chairs, n bloodied people.

He glances ma way, double taking as a sneer crosses his face. He moves towards us giving the 'come-ahead' sign with his fingers.

Ya fuckin beauty.

Judging by the way he holds himself, he's clearly handy, and has at least a stone advantage.

We meet just outta range and circle each other.

The surrounding chaos fades. It's like being in the eye of a tornado. There's only us two in the world. Fuck-all else matters. Pure nirvana.

His lead foot darts forward followed by a stiff jab.

Ah slip n parry the blow.

He smiles n nods.

Ma turn tae put the feelers oot. Ah faint like ah'm gonny shoot for his legs.

He squares n widens his stance, makes a cross guard wae his arms.

Ah flash him a cheeky wink.

He double steps towards us, throws a straight kick that just connects wae ma stomach, n rains a torrent ay blows at ma head.

A few glancing blows connect as ah slip back outta range. This boy can throw a dig. Wouldnae like tae catch one flush, so ah shoot for his legs, slam him ontae his back, n scramble intae the mount.

He knows wit's comin n covers up.

Ah rain hammer-fists ontae his head.

He's flailing like a bucking bronco, tryin tae throw us off.

No chance, kiddo. You're well and truly fucked n—

BOOM!

The winds took fae us n ah'm face down getting pounded fae behind. ma assailant lets up as somebody roars, 'GET FUCKIN AFF UM!'

Ah roll over. Another bouncer is stepping away fae us looking sheepish. The head bouncer gives him the evils before turnin tae me.

'Sorry aboot that, pal. I'll be havin words wae him later. Round two?'

Ah smile n get up, stretch a kink outta ma back.

Fuck.

'Games a bogey,' ah say.

A puzzled look crosses ma playmate's face. 'Eh?'

Ah signal behind him. 'Coppers.'

He snorts. 'Do ah look like ah wis born yesterday?'

'Straight up.' Ah hold ma hands up n step back, already scoping for a way out. 'Look.'

He glances over his shoulder, sees the stream ay police rushing in – batons n pepper spray in their hands. 'Argh, for fuck sake. Who fuckin phoned they cunts?'

He holds a clenched fist out. Ah bump it n he says, 'Come and see me if yer ever lookin for any work. Ask anybody in this toon for Big Geordie, and ye'll get pointed in the right direction.' He turns n heads for the coppers.

Ma eyes dart around the hall, but there's nae time tae marvel at the fruits ay ma labour. Ah'm needin a ticket outta here pronto.

Bingo!

The blonde haired, short-skirted lassie stood at the edge ay the battlefield will do nicely. Ah near sprint towards her.

'Do us a favour, doll.'

Her blue eyes meet mine, drop tae ma cheek for a split-second, before back tae ma eyes. 'Wit *kinda* favour?'

'Walk us outta here so's ah don't get lifted?'

'Em...'

'Ye got a boyfriend or that?'

'No,' she says quickly.

'Then wit's the problem?'

She rolls her eyes n sighs as if she doesnae want to. 'Fine.' She holds out a fake-tanned hand that's covered in costume jewellery. Mrs fuckin T, right here.

'Yer a wee star.' Ah grab her hand n head for the exit.

She sees us out the hall n all the way tae ma motor withoot lettin go ay ma hand, even though ah'm barely holdin hers.

'Nice car,' she says.

'Ah know. Jump in, I'll take ye for a spin.'

She bites her bottom duck-lip n glances around. 'Probably shouldn't. Ma pals'll be wondering where I am.'

'Probably' tells us she's nibbling on ma line. Don't want tae risk yanking the hook oot afore she swallows the lot. 'Don't then,' ah say, soundin like ah don't give a fuck. Which technically isnae far fae the truth.

Ah open the door n jump in. She stands there, bouncin on her toes fae the nervous energy surging through her. Folk always say the eyes betray our emotions. Pish. It's all in the legs. And ah wouldnae mind being all in *between* they legs, know wit ah mean? Ah start the motor, put it intae gear, n begin movin away.

KA-THUNK

The interior light comes on, and ah step on the brake. She jumps in n pulls the seat belt around herself.

'Wit aboot yer pals?' ah say.

'Just drive before I change my mind.'

'As ye wish, doll. As. You. Wish.'

* * *

'BLAH, BLAH, BLAH.'

Ah've been drivin aimlessly, listenin tae the tidy-wee-bit-ay-gear gibberin away next tae us. Well, *pretendin* tae listen would be a more accurate statement. These types ay birds are only interested in talkin about one thing – themselves. Apart fae askin ma name, she's no bothered diggin deeper. No that ah'd divulge any info if she did ask. Birds love mysterious men. Brings oot the natural nosey-bastard in them.

Kasabian's 'Reason is Treason' plays in the background while ah periodically nod n say general terms like, 'aye' n 'ah know', n laugh when the moment feels right. But ma mind's elsewhere. Ah'm reliving the night's exploits. It could not have gone better. Ah'm buzzin like a jar ay wasps. These things have more ups n downs than a cunt wae bipolar disorder doing a bungee jump – fear, excitement, trepidation, euphoria.

Imagine this universal scenario. It's the last day of yer summer holidays fae work. The last two weeks have flew in, and are now a hazy blur in yer mind. The day's been like drinkin a deadly cocktail ay dread n desperation, leavin a yucky feelin in the pit ay yer stomach. Ye go tae bed much earlier than ye had been during the last two weeks, and lie awake like a wean on Christmas eve. Except it's no nervous excitement keeping ye awake. Far from it. It's the absolute soul-crushing knowledge that tomorrow, it's back tae the grind. Back doing what, as a wean, ye never imagined ye'd spend the rest ay yer life doing. But life oftentimes kicks ye square in the baws. Ye glance at the clock on yer mobile n the terror ay the witching hour twists yer stomach.

Now, let me be clear, ah'm no speakin tae the lucky few who've found a way tae make a living doing wit they love. No. Ah'm speakin tae the vast majority of humanity that are slowly suffocatin. Hiding their crushed dreams like an ex-fatty hides stretch marks. The one's hurtling

210

towards the grave one paycheck, twelve-hour shift, early mornin alarm call at a time.

Now imagine jolting awake. Darkness shrouds yer room. Blankness shrouds yer mind. It's pure bliss. Ye think yer still on holiday n cannot wait tae go oot on yer jet-ski. You know, the one ye were just dreamin aboot. Then it's snap back-tae-reality n that sinkin feeling drags ye fae yer high thoughts. Ye slowly reach for yer phone, praying it's got some good news. Ye press the button on the side n the clock lights up – 05:35.

Fuckin dancer!

There's still nearly two whole hours before ye have tae face the enemy within n drag yer carcass out yer pit. Two hours ay pure, comforting bliss. Ye pull the covers tight under yer chin, let oot a contented sigh, n drift off tae that place where ye can be anything or anyone, hoping yer jet-ski's fuelled n ready tae go.

Multiply these riot ay emotions by ten. That's wit it's like. Pure unadulterated blissful euphoric power. Ye feel invincible. Bulletproof. Untouchable. Much like how auld Bill Must've felt gettin his dick sucked in the oval office.

And before ye get aw judgemental, stop n take a long hard look at yourself. This is a vice. ma vice, n everycunt has their own. Yours is likely sitting right next tae ye, beeping n vibrating for yer attention. Or it could be a rumble in yer belly that only gets satiated by junk food. Maybe it's the bottle ay pills yer GP pushes ontae ye that gets ye through the day. Perhaps ye have a hard drive ye would absolutely *hate* for the polis tae get ahold of. Whatever it is, we've all got our weaknesses. So, tae put it bluntly, ye can fuck off n ride yer high-horse elsewhere.

Speakin ay vices, this bird's barely peeled her eyes fae her own. Used tae be we'd look up in awe at the infinite, twinkling, light-show above and wonder. Now oor attention's been pulled doon. We now hang our heads in apathy at the infinite, twinkling, shit-show in our hands.

Keeps us fae lookin up n asking questions, ah suppose.

'Oh. My. God.' She cocks her head in ma direction. 'The riot's all over social media already.' She thrusts her phone in front ay ma face. 'See.'

Ah shake ma head. 'Terrible thing, that.'

'Says the guy wae the blood-stained shirt.'

Poker face engaged. 'Self defence, n all that jazz.'

'Ha! Is that what ye would've pleaded if I didn't rescue ye?'

'That or insanity.'

'Well, it definitely *was* insane. I was like *so* scared. Did you see that one Gypo jump from the ring into the Bikers? I've never seen anything like it. I didn't think I'd make it out alive. I—'

Me, me, me, me, me, me, me. 'Well ye did. And here ye are.'

'Here I am.'

'So, where to?'

'Where you off to?'

'Home.'

She pauses before askin, 'Fancy going for a drink?'

'Ah don't drink.'

'What, no even water?'

'Smart arse, you are. Ah'm no thirsty then.'

'Oh,' she says.

'So, where to?'

'Is yours an option?' she says, all shy n nervous like spunk wouldnae melt in her mouth.

Ah smile. 'If ye ask me, Ah'd say it's the best one there is.'

We're at mine quicker than the Pope runnin through Ibrox Stadium on matchday. Ah show her intae the living room n switch on the lights.

'Nice rug,' she says.

'Ah know. It's Himalayan pygmy-llama fur.'

She nods. 'Fancy.'

'That it is, ma wee saving grace. That it is.' Ah stick the tunes on – some chilled-oot, romantic playlist. 'Would the lady like some wine?'

'Thought you didnae drink?'

'Ye thought right.'

'Then why have ye got wine?' she says, aw smug like Columbo solvin this week's crime.

'Same reason ah've got coffee but don't drink coffee. Or tea bags but don't drink tea. So would you like some wine?'

'What are the options?'

'Aye or naw. It's no fuckin celebrity come dine with me.'

She laughs. 'Well fuckin aye then.'

Ah head intae ma kitchen, pullin ma phone oot as ah go and openin ma CCTV app. Ah press 'Living Room' on the main menu, and select 'Camera One' fae the drop-doon tab. A live stream ay ma livin room fills ma phone screen.

As ah'm pourin her wine n ma water, she's undressing in ma living room. She sniffs her oxters before rifling through her bag and spraying some perfume on. She then skooshes some breath freshener intae her mouth, breathes intae the palm ay her hand and gives it a sniff, before lying doon on the 'Himalayan pygmy-llama fur' rug. Nothin but aqua-blue, skimpy underwear and a seductive look on her. And of course, a fuck-ton ay makeup n fake tan.

They always want tae fuck on the 'exotic' rug.

Looks like diner'll have tae wait till breakfast. Ah stick the tubful ay scran ah'd made earlier intae the fridge, n grab the tub ay raw chicken fae it. The cool, night air floods ma kitchen when ah open the backdoor tae throw the meat intae ma garden. It's more than ah'd usually put oot for ma wee pal, but she'll be needing the extra. And it's no because she's got her pronouns on her unsocial media that ah know it's a she, but because the other night ah saw her wae two cubs. Tiny wee things wae big bushy tails. Ah think that wis their first venture fae their den.

Ah close the door, hit record on the CCTV app, grab the glasses, n head intae ma living room. These daddy issues urnae gonny fuck themselves.

* * *

BUBBLE BUBBLE CLICK

After showering, ah made a pot ay tea n coffee. Ah stick the two pots on a tray along wae a mug, jug ay milk, n bowl ay sugar, before headin back intae ma bedroom. Even though ah'd left her sleepin on the rug, ah woke early-doors tae find her snoring like a bear next tae us. Fuckin typical. If ah don't nip this in the bud she'll have her toothbrush in ma toilet, and her interior-designer skills everywhere else.

Ah set the tray on the bedside cabinet wae a bang. She jolts awake, wide-eyed before the realisation hits her.

'Morning,' she says wae a smile n a stretch.

'Good morning to you,' ah say, aw cheesy.

Ah drop the bath towel wrapped around ma waist, n stroll tae ma chest ay drawers.

'Wheeet-wheew!' she says. 'There's a sight for sore eyes.'

Ah can almost hear the squelch-squelch of her fanny juice. Ah slip on some boxers n head tae ma wardrobe.

'Awww, come back tae bed.'

'I'd love to, but duty calls.' Ah put the troosers on.

'Wit do ye mean?'

Ah slip the t-shirt over ma head n turn. 'Ah need tae go tae work.'

The disappointment on her face quickly turns tae shock as her eyes fall on the big, golden 'M' on ma t-shirt. The fanny-juice torrent recedes.

'You don't work in McDonalds.'

'Jesus, we've no even been going out a full day, n you're already trying tae boss us about.'

Her mouth opens wide as her fanny juice now drips. 'But...'

'But what?'

'...It's just...no wit I expected.'

'Wit *did* ye expect? A super-sized seagull?'

'No, I just thought, wae the way yer house is kitted out n yer motor, ye must've had a good job. Or at the very least, be a drug dealer.'

Ah feign insult. 'Is there somethin wrong wae workin in McDonald's?'

'Not if yer sixteen there's no.' The realisation that she knows fuck all about us – a guy who, not a million years ago, wis uptae his nuts in her guts – is announced by a look ay horror creeping across her face. 'How old *are* you anyway?'

'How old do ye think ah am?'

She scowls n sits up, pulls the covers around herself. 'Don't play games.'

That's rich coming fae her. 'Ah never play games. That's why ah'm trying tae be honest with ye the now. Start as ye mean tae go on, as they say.'

The fanny juice tap gets turned off. 'Ye weren't honest with me last night.'

'Really? Wit aboot?'

'Everything!'

'Everything?'

'Aye, everything about you.'

'Ah don't recall ye askin.'

'That's no the point. Last night ye were acting like Pablo. Now I see it was all a show. How do ye even get all this stuff flippin burgers in

McDonald's?'

'Well first off all, ah don't flip burgers, unless of course somebody's phoned in sick, which is usually every Saturday n Sunday. Ah'm the manager. Well, assistant manager. And second, this isnae ma hoose.'

'Who's house is it?'

'Ma pal's. He works offshore n lets us stay here when he's away.'

'Where *do* ye live?'

'Eh...the truth is, ah'm currently between houses.'

'Yer fuckin *homeless?*'

Ah fight tae keep a straight face as the fanny-juice authorities declare a drought.

'Aye,' ah say, rubbin the back ay ma neck. 'But ma pals no back for another two months. All going well between us, we could maybe get a wee place of our own by then.'

'I've got a boyfriend.'

There it is – an exit strategy formulated. 'What? But you said last night—'

'I know, I know,'—like a lobster in a pot, she's scramblin for a way out—'what I meant was, I've no *actually* got a boyfriend, but I've been seeing this guy, and I'd like to see where it goes.'

Good save. Gordon Banks would be proud. 'Oh. Right.'

'I'm sorry for no being straight up with you, but I'd had a shitload to drink.'

'Nah, it's cool.' Ah let the awkwardness linger. 'Well, do ye fancy going for breakfast? Could go tae ma work before the start ay ma shift. Would be a freebie. Perks ay the job, n all that.'

'I need to go.' Her eyes dart around ma bedroom. 'Where's ma clothes?'

Ah think this lassie's just started the menopause. 'In the living room. I'll get them for—'

'It's fine.' She stands, wraps the covers around herself, n waddles out ma room.

'Wit aboot lunch?' ah call.

'No!'

Ah slap a palm over ma mouth as ma belly chortles wae laughter.

After using ma toilet, she's oot the door without so much as a cheerio. It's like ma brother used tae say – snakes wae tits.

Ah take the tray back intae ma kitch—

DING-DONG!

Fuck. She'd better no have had a change ay heart. Ah creep tae ma front door n peer through the keek-hole. Thank fuck. This is one bird ah don't mind seeing again.

Ah open the door n fling ma arms oot wide. 'Jean! Ya GILF n a half.'

She barges past, trailin her shoppin cart behind her. 'I'll GILF ye, son. You'll be getting nowhere near me after seeing what's just dragged itself out your door.' She stops n looks us up n doon – a puzzled look across her wrinkled coupon. 'What's wae the uniform? Are you doing community service, or is this some kinky role-play fantasy yous young-yins are doing?'

'Aye,' ah say, 'it's called the burger and the buns. You've got them fine buns n ah would love tae burger them!'

'Ah-ha-ha-ha-ha!'

She leaves her shopping cart at the door n follows us intae ma living room. Ah pick up the covers strewn across the floor n fling them behind the couch.

'Aw son, please tell me ye didnae make that poor lassie sleep on the couch. No wonder her face was like thunder.'

'Wit can ah say, Jean. You're the only bird that's good enough tae share ma bed.' Ah flash her a wink and a cheeky smile.

'Even if I was forty years younger, you'd be ontae plums.'

Ah clutch ma chest. 'Ouch! That cut deep.'

She laughs n waves her hand dismissively.

Ah signal tae ma couch. 'Make yourself at home.'

She lets out a groan as she plunks herself doon.

'Is your arthritis playing up?' ah ask.

'No, no, son. Just stiffness in the auld legs. Word of advice – don't get old.'

Ah nod. 'I've just boiled the kettle. Can ah get ye a tea or a coffee?'

'No thanks, son, I'll no be staying long. I'm away round to our Stephen's. They've got a christening this morning. Said I'd watch their Rebecca, you know, their newborn, so's they get a bit of peace. Only thing worse than going to church is having a screaming bairn tae shush while you're there.'

'Aye, you'd mentioned Stef wis gonny be a father. Never knew they'd had the wean, though. How is the wee one?'

'Aw, son, she's an absolute wee cracker, she really is. She's the double of Stephen when he wis a bairn.'

'Fingers crossed she'll grow outta it.'

She shakes her head n tuts. 'Ya cheeky bugger, ye.'

'Ah'm only joking, Jean. Auld Stef always was a looker. The lassies at school were forever glancin his way. Tell him ah'm askin for him, will ye?'

'Will do, son.' She opens her handbag n pulls out a wee empty jam-jar. 'Ah don't mean to be rude, but I really need to get going.' She hands us the jar n pulls her purse out. 'How much is a quarter again?'

To most cunts it's sixty quid. 'Twenty quid.'

She pulls a wad ay notes fae her purse.

'Fuck me, Jean, have you been oan the rob?'

She laughs. 'No, no, son. This is ma pension. Gets paid into ma bank every Friday, but I lift it out as soon as possible. I trust they bankers about as far as I can throw them.' She slips a twenty off the wad n hands us it.

'Here, here. In the hierarchy ay folk I'd like tae see hangin fae their crown jewels, they come a close second tae paedos.'

She laughs.

'Just watch wit yer doing wae aw that cash. There's too many torags walkin they streets.'

'I might be an auld woman, but I'm certainly no stupid.' There's a wee, mischievous twinkle in they ancient green-eyes.

'Ah don't doubt that for a second.'

'Plus, it's no as if they'd get a lot from me. State pensions are no exactly pop-star wages.'

Ah shake ma head. 'It's a bloody disgrace.'

'You're right, son. Ye spend all yer days working hard and contribut-ing, then when it's your time to put yer feet up, the buggers want none of it, and would rather see ye carted off to the glue factory.'

'It's pish, Boxer. It's absolutely pish.' Ah rub ma chin. 'Listen, Jean, if ye want—'

'No, no, son, I'm no here begging. Just telling how it is. I'm no trying to guilt ye into giving me free stuff.'

Ah smile. 'Ah wouldn't even try.'

'Don't kid a kidder. I know ye always give me more than what I pay for. Do ye think I've no got scales?'

Ah feign insult. 'So, ye weigh ma stuff after ye get home? Ah must no have a trustworthy face.'

'The only trustworthy face is the one ye see in the mirror. And even that one can betray ye sometimes.'

'That's exactly wit ma brother used tae say.'

A seriousness descends upon her face. 'How long has he been...gone for now, son? Must be about fifteen years.'

Why the fuck did ah bring him up? 'Eh...Too long, Jean. Too long.'

'Aye, just when he was starting to sort himself out as well.'

Time tae wrap this up. 'I'll no keep ye anymore. Give us two minutes.' Ah turn n head for the kitchen.

Ah dig oot a jar ay weed. No the shitey mouldy stuff – the Gucci gear – and eyeball a quarter intae the jam jar she gave us. Then ah add some more. Ah bury the twenty-pound note in among the buds, n screw the lid on tight, making sure the note's hidden before headin back tae the living room, hoping Jean doesnae mention anythin else about ma brother.

1

---

[1] To continue reading *The Great Divider*, keep an eye out on your poison of choice for release updates. Links can be found here: linkr.bio/eviscopet

About the Author

Peter is a six-foot-ten goth who works at Brownings and calls himself The Underbaker. He's spun waltzers at the shows, guarded bonfires from the council, sold Avon for yer da, punted cooncil for yer maw, been an offshore tree surgeon, apprentice bingo caller, sign language interpreter at The Royal Blind School, and doctored a logbook entry or two in his time. He's also yer gran's favourite author. For the pedantic literalists – he writes FICTION. Hate mail and sanctimonious pearl-clutching may be directed below.

You can connect with me on:

🌐 https://www.notsotalltaleteller.com

🔗 https://linkr.bio/eviscopet

🔗 https://www.goodreads.com/book/show/59683252-only-a-fool-sleeps-in-the-shadow-of-a-camel-s-back?ac=1&from_search=true&qid=nzHacKfx8l&rank=4

Printed in Great Britain
by Amazon

71761731R00139